D0130758

THE ANIMAL RESCUE AGENCY

Case File: Pangolin Pop Star

Also by **ELIOT SCHREFER**

The Animal Rescue Agency: Case File: Little Claws

The Lost Rainforest: Mez's Magic
The Lost Rainforest: Gogi's Gambit
The Lost Rainforest: Rumi's Riddle

THE ANIMAL RESCUE AGENCY

Case File: Pangolin Pop Star

BY **ELIOT SCHREFER**

ILLUSTRATED BY
DANIEL DUNCAN

KATHERINE **T**EGEN **B**OOK*s*
An Imprint of HarperCollins Publishers

Katherine Tegen Books is an imprint of HarperCollins Publishers.

The Animal Rescue Agency: Case File: Pangolin Pop Star
Text copyright © 2022 by Schrefer LLC
Illustrations copyright © 2022 by Daniel Duncan
All rights reserved. Printed in the United States of America.
No part of this book may be used or reproduced in any manner whatsoever without
written permission except in the case of brief quotations embodied in critical articles
and reviews. For information address HarperCollins Children's Books, a division of
HarperCollins Publishers, 195 Broadway, New York, NY 10007.
www.harpercollinschildrens.com

ISBN 978-0-06-298236-0

Typography by Andrea Vandergrift
22 23 24 25 26   PC/LSCH   10 9 8 7 6 5 4 3 2 1

First Edition

For Patty

Jewel the pangolin had been having the most wonderful dream. She'd been lost in the trees, surrounded by so many shades of green, so many humming insects and chirping frogs. Her sharp front claws had broken open a crumbly log, and inside were fat ants. Slurp, slurp, slurp with her long tongue, and down they went.

It turned out she'd been slurping her pillow. When she opened her eyes, she saw the silk was covered in goo from her sticky saliva. How unclassy. Jewel delicately turned the pillow over. There, no one would notice.

She pressed her claws over her eyes and tried to live inside the dream for a few more minutes. She didn't

remember ever visiting a
place like that, but the last
few nights she'd dreamed of
the same jungle. So many
leaves (and delicious
ants!) in one place.
Where had this fan-
tasy land come from?
As far as she could remember, her
life had been only private jets and fancy hotels.

Jewel looked around to see if anyone had spotted
her drooling, but the resort hotel room was empty.
How strange. Her beloved owner—Dizzy Dillinger,
the biggest human pop star in the world—wasn't there.
His other exotic pets, Butch the wildcat and Arabella
the monkey, weren't there. Neither was Jewel's brother,
Beatle.

Where *was* everyone?

Then Jewel looked out of the villa's window and
saw that the sun, which she thought really ought to be
up at the top of the sky, was closer to the horizon, turning the sea orange.

She was late!

On instinct Jewel rolled into a tight ball, her scales
sticking out everywhere. But that was no help—that

strategy was for predators! Not that her dear Dizzy would ever let her get near any of those. Jewel unrolled herself, whiskers trembling, then scampered off the silk pillow and out the door. "You're a star," she scolded herself. "You better act like it."

She got her nerves under control and stepped haughtily down the corridor. Dizzy Dillinger always insisted that his pets be allowed to freely roam whatever resort he was staying in. The hallway was all a blur—everything was always a blur to Jewel, actually, with her weak pangolin eyes—but it was full of smells that gave a lot of information to her sensitive nose. She could detect Caribbean seawater on the other side of the billowing curtains, the fragrance of the individual ants marching through the walls, and the scent of humans all around. That was Dizzy's friends and road crew, preparing for his big concert that weekend.

She easily tracked her brother's fragrance, following it through the hallways, calmly stepping between human legs all the while. One particularly awkward-looking human tried to pet her. (Ew! No way!) Finally she climbed a staircase banister to get to Beatle's dressing room.

Before she went in, she double-checked that there was no more drool crusted on the tip of her nose. Her brother teased her whenever she looked less than per-fect.

Beatle's dressing room was what a human would have called a cosmetics trunk, but Dizzy's pets knew it was much more than that. Inside was a paradise of colors. One side was covered top to bottom in bottles of nail polish, a rainbow of blueberries and lemons and plums. Beatle had a strawberry-red bottle in one claw and was delicately applying the color to the smallest scales at the tip of his tail.

The polish was a big reason for Beatle's fame in the animal world. He spent hours painting himself before each concert or even a dress rehearsal, like tonight. It was an amazing effect, which was why his concerts drew even bigger crowds than Dizzy's. (To be fair, any-time roaches and rabbits are invited to an event, the attendance numbers get very big very quickly.)

"You're late, sister," Beatle snapped. "My Indigo Inten-sity scales are still going to be wet during the rehearsal."

"I'm sorry, Beatle!" Jewel said, casting her eyes to the black velvet at the bottom of the trunk. "I was hav-ing that dream again, the one with all the trees and the frogs and the bugs—"

"Hurry up," Beatle interrupted. "The bottle's over there."

"I thought you loved this part of the day," Jewel grumbled. Her brother was the only creature in her life that dared to order her around. She picked up the polish in her front claws, her sensitive nose wrinkling at its harsh scent. Beatle liked to do most of his rainbow himself, but he couldn't reach the scales behind his neck. Those were his sister's responsibility.

She held her breath as she stroked Indigo Intensity between her brother's shoulders. "It looks just as beautiful as always," she said.

In the good old days, her brother would have sighed and asked her to fetch a mirror so he could admire the color, and they would have oohed and aahed for a while. But lately he'd become so irritable. "Don't forget, it's turn-turn-shuffle during the new chorus, not turn-shuffle-turn," he said.

"Yep, don't worry, I've got it," Jewel said. "You forget you're talking to the best backup dancer in the whole animal kingdom. Now stop wiggling, or you're going to smear Indigo Intensity all over your Cornflower Morning."

"Sorry, sis," Beatle said. "It's just that everyone's expecting a perfect show from me. These animals are coming from so far away. It's a lot of pressure."

"You and Dizzy are definitely two of a kind," Jewel

said, shaking her head. "Your shows are always perfect, but you always worry yourself miserable about them."

Beatle let out a long sigh. Jewel almost asked him to explain what was on his mind, but then Beatle briskly shivered his scales and shook a bottle of see-through polish. "I set some Crystal Clear aside for you."

"That's okay, I'm just the backup dancer, I don't need any polish for the rehearsal. *You're* the star."

Beatle smiled, clearly feeling a little better. This was a routine that they did before every performance, where she worked up his confidence. "I wish we didn't have to keep our shows hidden from humans like Dizzy," Beatle said, carefully slotting the nail polish into the rack. "I bet he'd be proud of us."

"No one will be proud of you if you're late to your own dress rehearsal. Come on!" Jewel said. She climbed out of the cosmetics trunk, crawled up some nearby curtains, and dropped out an open window.

Beatle plopped to the sandy ground beside her, shaking his claws. "I just put on this Creamsicle Orange, and it's already getting covered in sand. That stuff is everywhere around here."

"I know, it's a tragedy," Jewel said. "Poor you, suffering on a private island in the Bahamas."

"If the animals see anything imperfect, they'll be

disappointed," Beatle sniffed. "Let's try to find me disposable booties to wear before the actual concert, so I don't look like a clod of sand out there."

Dizzy Dillinger was hosting a weeklong party on his island, with fancy humans sailing in on their yachts for his concert on the last evening. As usual, Beatle would copy Dizzy's schedule to the minute—with his own animal fans traveling in from all over the world. (Though they would be arriving by sea turtle and albatross instead of by yacht and private plane.)

As a backup dancer, Jewel knew that she wasn't feeling nearly the pressure that her brother was. "They're all here for your voice, not your Creamsicle Orange polish," she said. "Now, let's get a move on. The crew is waiting."

"What even is a Creamsicle?" Beatle asked.

"I have no idea," Jewel said. "Some human thing." She filled her nose with the scents of the outdoors. Most animals flocked to the area for the black-sand beaches and the baby-blue water, but for Jewel the beauties of the Caribbean were all the wonderful smells. Here the air was full of salt and pine, way better than the stale, dried-out odors of their pet suite.

The pangolin brother and sister picked their way along the sand and scrub, toward the rocky plateau.

There, the iguana roadies were checking the stage. They'd positioned the structure (actually a TV stand borrowed from a hotel room) on a rocky plateau over-looking the sea. For safety they were tying it to the rocks, leaving a crawl space beneath. The sun would set right behind Beatle as he gave his show, glinting off his multicolored scales and the waves beyond.

Butch the wildcat was sitting where the animal audi-ence would be for the actual concert, cleaning his glossy fur while he pretended not to watch the hutias rigging lights up in the bushes. The rodents were positioning and repositioning LEDs from the hotel's freebie key chains until they converged on the middle of the stage. Butch barely looked Beatle's and Jewel's way before returning to licking the striped fur between his thick claws. "I see you two have finally decided to join us."

"Maybe I was just building dramatic tension," Beatle sniffed.

"Talent on the set!" called a voice from a nearby palm tree. It was Arabella the monkey, the third of Dizzy Dillinger's exotic pets—and the show's director. "My whole family's on their way from Costa Rica to see the concert, you know that? Better be good! Don't embarrass me, okay?" She had something in her hand, which she bit into with gusto. She scowled and let it drop to the ground. "I thought that was a fig. It was definitely not a fig." She took out an old birthday hat, which she'd snipped the end off to make a monkey-sized megaphone. "Places, everyone! Let's get ready to make art!"

Beatle climbed to the center of the stage, stood up on his hind legs, and fanned his painted claws in front of his face. "How do I look?"

"Gorgeous as always," Jewel said as she took up her position at the rear. She noticed a circular cut in the stage, right around where Beatle was standing. "What's that?" she called.

"Arabella added an effect," Butch growled. "A platform is going to rise up in the middle of the first number. It's a little overdramatic if you ask me."

"Music! Start the music!" Arabella shrieked from the palms. "We can't have a show without music!"

One of the hutias tried to press the button on the portable speaker. Nothing happened. It tried leaping on it. Still nothing. Hutias don't have a lot of muscle.

Butch sighed. "I guess I have to do everything. As usual." The hutia scampered away as Butch padded over to the speaker and pressed a button. An electronic dance beat thudded out. "That sounds awful," Butch yelled over the noise. "Maybe you'll reconsider having a live band."

That "live band," of course, used to be Butch himself. He would pluck a harp and sing and bang a drum with his tail, all at the same time. It was . . . impressive. As in it made an impression. Of being painful to the ears. Now that Beatle had switched to recorded music, Butch's only responsibility was keeping guard.

"Three measures of lead-in!" Arabella called. "Places, pangolins. Five, six, seven, eight!"

Jewel's role was easy. She shuffled back and forth to the tempo of the electronica, shaking her hips and making her tail wave like a ribbon. Occasionally she sang, "ooh, ooh."

Her brother, though, really was breathtaking. His rainbow of nail polish reflected the light from the setting sun, making a sherbet smear of colors.

And that was before he opened his mouth to sing!

The closest sound to a pangolin's voice is wind chimes. The moment Beatle began to sing his number one hit, "Every Scale is Major," all the animals within earshot went still. Even Butch's tail relaxed, and his ears went back.

Jewel's brother really was talented. She had been

trying to convince him for years that his voice was enough; he didn't need to add rainbow scales and an electronic beat. But he always wanted to be improving so he wouldn't let everyone down.

This time, though, she found she wasn't able to concentrate on her brother's performance. The stage wobbled as she crossed back and forth. Just a little bit of tilt, but any wobble was too much when you were on top of a cliff. "Excuse me," she called to the nearest iguana roadie, "did you already test the stage?"

"What?" the iguana called back, cupping a claw behind his scaly ear. "I can't hear you!"

The reason he couldn't hear Jewel was that the music had reached its thundering climax. The circle beneath Beatle began to rumble. Instead of lifting, like Arabella had said it would, it began to sink!

"Stop the music!" Jewel shrieked.

The music continued to blare on as the platform sank even more.

As the trapdoor dropped beneath the stage, Beatle locked eyes with his sister. "Help me, Jewel!" he called.

She reached out for him. It felt like time had slowed, that she'd never reach her brother. As she got near, she saw his midsection disappear, and then his neck. For a moment her brother's head was there, and then it was . . . gone!

Jewel reached the edge of the trapdoor and peered down below. There was a giant gap in the rock, a crevasse leading far down into the earth. Her brother had disappeared down it. Completely vanished. "Beatle!" she cried.

She listened for a response but couldn't hear anything over the ruckus. "Cut the music!" she cried.

Butch turned off the electronica, and the evening air again filled with the chirping of the island cicadas. "Beatle?" Jewel tried again.

"I'm trapped down here!" came his voice. It was quiet, almost impossible to hear. He was very far away.

Arabella scampered to the edge and peered in, her eyes wide with astonishment. "You can hear him, with your super pangolin hearing?" she asked Jewel.

Jewel nodded. "He's way, way down this hole."

The rest of the animals approached in shocked silence. The iguana and hutia roadies, Arabella and Butch, every one of them struck dumb by what had happened.

How could the lift, which was supposed to send Beatle up into the air, have dropped him into this crevasse instead? "Beatle!" Jewel cried again.

She heard a soft scramble from far below, a yelp from Beatle, and then nothing. He must have fallen even deeper in.

Jewel's mind spun. In the corner of her brain, a thought was already forming.

They had to get Beatle out before he starved, or before the whole thing caved in. But how to manage that when he was deep down a hole?

She was in over her head.

She needed help.

And when an animal truly needed help, there was only one place to turn.

The Animal Rescue Agency.

Artist rendering of incident in Conch Group Iguana Parrot, Private island location of upcoming Dizzy Dillinger/Beatle the Pangolin concert. Biggest star in the animal world MISSING two days before concert. Please relay to Esquire Fox of the Animal Rescue Agency, ASAP. URGENT.

CHAPTER

"Up to the left, no, no, *up* to the left!" Mr. Pepper said. "Don't foxes know what *up* means?"

"Yes, Mr. Pepper, I understood the word. It's not a difficult word. But I've already *tried* it up to the left," Esquire replied through gritted teeth.

"Well, try it up there again."

Esquire lifted the piece of driftwood higher on the wall of the den. Now it would be near impossible for anyone to see it—which might be just what Mr. Pepper was going for. It was not the most beautiful piece of art ever to decorate the lair of the Animal Rescue Agency. Not by a long shot. But Little Claws was their newest field agent, and if he sent them a gift, then it had to go on display somewhere. He lived at the North Pole, which to hear him tell it was the most boring place in the world. So he'd taken up crafting, sending down "art" made from whatever scraps washed up north. The last gift he'd sent was a wet envelope with three rocks and two sticks inside. "Hope you enjoy this snowman!" the note had said.

The driftwood was high enough now that it was under the shadow of the ceiling, basically invisible. "That's perfect!" Mr. Pepper called.

"It's a very sweet gesture," Esquire said, climbing down the ladder and folding it up to slide neatly away under the couch. "I just wish Little Claws had more sense of our tastes."

"That piece of driftwood will be the closest we get to income from that cursed North Pole adventure," Mr. Pepper clucked, before straightening his strawberry apron with his beak.

Esquire wiped her paws on her waistcoat and held her tongue. She'd been going gently with Mr. Pepper ever since their arctic adventure. He'd nearly died after riding a walrus through freezing waves, and his arthritis had been flaring up ever since. Not that Mr. Pepper would ever admit that. But Esquire knew.

The Animal Rescue Agency might have agents around the globe, ready to spring into action the moment an animal relayed a distress signal to the headquarters, but it couldn't operate without Mr. Pepper taking care of the details. Esquire was well aware of that!

He resumed his daily cleaning of the bookshelves, which involved bursting into the air and dusting a few square inches before he floated back to the ground, then repeating the process all over again.

Esquire stood back in her moccasins and peered up at the driftwood, tapping her claw against the tip of her nose. "I wonder if we might establish an art rotation system. That octopus promised to send us an amphora;

remember that? And I honestly can't think where we'll put—oh my!"

Up high on the den wall was a box with two lights. They read Incoming Animal Distress Calls and Extra Urgent. The first one was lit.

Well. At least it wouldn't be a high-stakes rescue this time. "Incoming call, Mr. Pepper," Esquire said. "I hope you're all caught up with your dusting."

She eased into her desk chair and jiggled the mouse to wake up her computer. A notification window filled the screen. She read it over, then bounded out of the desk chair. "Oh, Mr. Pepper!" she exclaimed. "Good news. It's not an emergency after all. We've been invited to a party!"

Esquire Fox, please come join us in Conch Grouper Iguana Parrot, location of upcoming Beatle the Pangolin concert. ASAP. URGENT.

"Really?" he clucked. "Let me see that. We're never invited to parties. Only to rescues."

"And don't I know it! But look—it's right here, clear as day," Esquire said, tapping the screen triumphantly. "'Esquire Fox, please come join us in ConchGrouperIguanaParrot, private island location of upcoming Beatle the Pangolin concert. ASAP. URGENT.' See? We're off to the Bahamas, Mr. Pepper!"

"Don't tap the screen with your claws. It's not designed for foxes. And *urgent*? What kind of party invite ends with the word *urgent*?"

"An amazing one!" Esquire said, clapping her paws. "They want us there *that much*. I love Beatle the Pangolin's music. I didn't know he knew about us—our fame must be increasing. We have to get packing!"

"And what kind of party invite triggers the distress light in the den?" Mr. Pepper asked, tilting his head so far back that his coxcomb wiggled.

"It's a technical glitch, I'm sure. Oh, Mr. Pepper, it doesn't matter, because we're going to the *beach*. There will be sun and sand and no polar ice caps whatsoever."

Mr. Pepper stretched out his clawed foot, trying to massage the pain out of the digits. "Being someplace warm does sound nice."

"I've got that bathing suit I made out of the leg of a

wet suit. Do you remember where I put it?"

"Second drawer from the top of the chest of drawers," Mr. Pepper said. "But you are *not* wearing clothing on this trip. Don't you remember how that tweed jacket of yours nearly got us killed in the Arctic?"

Esquire had already whisked the drawer open and was rummaging through. Gloves, waistcoats, and tiny woolen socks all went flying while she thought about her friend's words. "Is the real problem maybe that you don't have anything to wear at the beach, Mr. Pepper?"

"Preposterous. I will not be bathing. Chickens do not bathe."

"Why not? You did in the Arctic, and this time the water will be so much warmer."

"Chickens do not swim," Mr. Pepper said. Suddenly Esquire figured out what was troubling him. The invitation hadn't mentioned Mr. Pepper at all.

She made her way to their other dresser, the one with her private drawer. Standing on her tiptoes, she rummaged around until she'd found a tissue-wrapped bundle.

She kneeled in front of Mr. Pepper and held it out.

"What's happening?" he asked suspiciously.

"It's a *present*, Mr. Pepper. Just open it. I got it for you a long time ago, and I would have brought it to the

Bahamas to give to you there, but I think that maybe you'd like to see it right now."

"You know I don't like surprises," Mr. Pepper said. All the same, he was the picture of focus as he worked a clawed foot beneath the dried sap sealing the package. "Oh my," he said once he'd revealed what was beneath.

"Do you like it?!" Esquire asked.

Mr. Pepper grasped a piece of fabric in his beak and unfurled it. His present.

It was a quilted handbag. Or it *had* been a quilted handbag, until Esquire had removed the straps and handles and snipped a hole in the top. Now it looked like one of those old-timey bathing suits that humans used to wear a hundred years ago. Only sized for a chicken. And maybe not waterproof? Hmm.

"Thank you, Esquire," Mr. Pepper said, his voice neutral.

"You're not going to try it on?"

"As I said, chickens do not go bathing. That means chickens do not wear bathing suits. Generally. Most animals shouldn't wear clothing. Generally."

"We'll bring it," Esquire said gently. "And if you decide to use it, that will make me very happy. But you're under no pressure."

Mr. Pepper held very still, staring at the bathing suit like it was a coiled snake.

"I really do adore Beatle the Pangolin's music," Esquire said cheerily, slamming the drawer closed with a back paw as she crossed the room, socks piled in her paws. "A Bahamas concertgoing outfit, I wonder what that should be, hmm. And Mr. Pepper, do you know where my—"

"Suitcase with the brass fasteners is?" Mr. Pepper finished, still staring at his present, soaking up every detail.

"No, actually, I was thinking of that beachy linen duffel bag."

"I'm using it to store the spare dish towels. You'll have to empty it out if you want to use it."

While Esquire emptied the duffel bag, she cut

glances at Mr. Pepper. He was still looking at the bathing suit, nudging it this way and that with his foot. She'd get him to enjoy this vacation; she was sure of it.

She merrily went about her packing, while Mr. Pepper went quiet, scrutinizing every detail of his new bathing suit.

They were both so preoccupied that neither noticed that the second bulb on the display had lit up. The one that read Extra Urgent.

CHAPTER

They traveled down to Miami by sneaking a ride on a freight train, then completed their journey by sea turtle. "I say we travel by turtle from here on out," Esquire resolved, perched high on the beast's sloping back.

The sea surrounding them was crystal blue, the waves were calm, and the only thing to be seen on the horizon were white-sand islands feathered with bright green foliage. Myrtle the sea turtle was doing a magnificent job keeping her back above water, so Esquire and Mr. Pepper didn't have to worry about falling into the ocean.

Even so, the rooster was keeping right to the center

of Esquire's lap. "Only you could call trusting our lives to a stranger in the middle of the ocean a good idea," Mr. Pepper clucked.

Esquire patted the sea turtle's shell. "Myrtle's not a stranger! We had a lovely conversation back in South Beach. I feel like we're good friends already."

Myrtle didn't answer. She was too busy swimming.

"I'll be ready to get back on solid land, that's for sure," Mr. Pepper said, with a cross of his wings that Esquire knew meant he was done talking.

She removed her sunglasses (a paper pair, snagged from the dumpster behind a children's optometrist and dolled up with glitter) and lifted her binoculars to her eyes. "You're about to get your wish, Mr. Pepper."

Beneath the sun stretched a glittering beach, with an enormous yacht anchored at its farthest end. Esquire could make out humans milling on the deck—probably getting ready for the Dizzy Dillinger concert. At the other end of the island was a big resort, with multiple swimming pools and doorways and windows and balconies everywhere. Sweating humans, dressed all in black, were setting up a stage in the resort's driveway. "I guess that's where Dizzy's concert will be—but where will Beatle play?" Esquire wondered.

"As long as he's performing on dry land, it will be

fine by me," Mr. Pepper replied. "Ooh, I swear! A jelly-fish just stung me between my underfeathers!"

"There are no jellyfish on the back of this sea tur-tle," Esquire said, patting her friend on the top of his head. "And we're almost to the shore—oh, here we go!"

Myrtle came to rest on a sandbar, still a good two dozen feet from the beach. The turtle lifted her head above the waterline and craned her neck to fix them a look from one eye. "I'm not willing to go any farther. I'd rather not get near humans."

"Perfectly reasonable," Mr. Pepper said. "We'll be sure to check on your egg stash while we're here, just as you asked." He looked nervously down at the seawater.

"Thank you," Myrtle said. "It's much easier for a fox or a chicken to sneak along the beach. Even ones wear-ing funny clothing."

"Do you like the pattern on my jacket?" Esquire asked proudly. "I think the sunglasses really help coor-dinate it all."

"We will not be wearing these clothes for long," Mr. Pepper grumbled. "I'm not about to let you go get us trapped by an animal hunter again."

"Strong words from someone still wearing his strawberry apron. And I'll get you into that bathing suit before this is all out, too, Mr. Pepper," Esquire said, stepping off into the seawater. It went right up to her middle, soaking her tail. It was all delightfully cooling—her fur had crisped up in the sunshine. "We'll need to return in three days," she said to Myrtle. "Perhaps you'll be willing to take us back?"

"Of course. In the meantime, I'm going to find something that I can digest. I've been having trouble eating lately—I ate a crinkly jellyfish that disagreed with me."

"A crinkly jellyfish?" Mr. Pepper asked. "That doesn't sound right. Perhaps you'd let me look—"

But Myrtle didn't have the best hearing. She also couldn't feel anything on top of her shell and was already pushing up off the sandbar to return to sea. Mr. Pepper squawked as salt water began rising around his fluff.

Esquire plucked him from the turtle's back just in time, tucked him under one foreleg, and got their duffel under the other. She blew a gust up from her snout to stop her paper sunglasses from falling into the ocean, then started toward shore. It wasn't so easy making her way off the sandbar with sodden fur and forelegs fully loaded, but she managed to do it without soaking their luggage—or Mr. Pepper.

On the shore, a tiny figure came into view. Leg count—two. Wing count—two! Yep, that was

Alphonse, their regional agent. "Ahoy there!" Esquire exclaimed.

"Alphonse the bat, at your service!" he called back. Or at least Esquire thought he did. His voice was too high-pitched to carry well over the surf. But it was definitely him. Esquire's sharp vision could make out the unmistakable silver of the key ring he'd long ago decided was a belt.

"Our field agent is waiting for us, Mr. Pepper!" Esquire exclaimed.

"Yes, I heard you. Less talking and more wading, please," Mr. Pepper said, staring into the waves.

Once she'd reached the beach, Esquire set the duffel and Mr. Pepper down on the hot sand and put her paws on her hips, looking around triumphantly. "Gorgeous. This will do fine!"

Alphonse gave an elaborate bow, his key ring belt falling around his little bat feet as he did. Blushing, he pulled it back up. "Esquire! Mr. Pepper! I'm glad this rescue has brought you our way!"

"Well, that's the thing," Esquire said proudly. "This isn't a rescue at all. It's a party!"

Mr. Pepper held up a wing to silence her even as he hopped from one foot to the other on the scalding sand.

"Unless you have different information, Alphonse?"

The bat turned somber and gestured along the beach with one of his wings. "Perhaps we can walk and talk. We have no time to lose."

"Of course," Esquire said, her fizzy feelings rapidly flattening as she and Mr. Pepper started along the beach.

"Dizzy Dillinger's guards patrol the island every two hours," Alphonse said. "They're due to come around in about twenty minutes or so, so we need to get hidden away in the villa by then."

"Yes, we'll be sure to," Esquire said, adjusting her sunglasses.

As she sped along the beach her mind rumbled along in its distracted Esquire way, and she was on her fifth or sixth thought when she realized that Alphonse hadn't said anything in a while. She turned around to find him well behind them, struggling to catch up on his little brown legs. "Sorry!" she called. "Maybe you'd like to ride on my shoulder?"

"That would be nice, thank you," Alphonse said, panting. "I don't fly during the day; there are too many predatory birds out there. And this sand is quite hot."

After Esquire had placed the bat on her shoulder,

they continued off again. "Much better," Alphonse said. "Thank you. I was one of the messengers who helped relay the distress signal that reached your den. An iguana caught me up right when I arrived for Beatle's concert, and I passed the news to a piping plover to get back to the mainland. The trouble all started at the dress rehearsal."

"Was there not enough bass on the speaker?" Esquire asked. "I always like lots of bass."

"I'm afraid it's much more serious than that," Alphonse said sadly. "Beatle the Pangolin has gone missing."

Esquire turned somber. Whether it had started as a party invite or not, this was now a rescue mission after all. "What do we know?"

"Not very much. He disappeared during the dress rehearsal. The lift that was supposed to raise him in the air dropped him into a deep crevasse instead. His sister heard from him for a few moments, but nothing since. I would suggest you start by interviewing Jewel. She was closest to him when the incident occurred."

"Did you say *incident*, not *accident*?" Esquire asked, looking up to the cliffside.

"Yes," Alphonse said sadly. "We would be foolish

not to consider foul play. As I see it there are three suspects, all with equally compelling motives to make Beatle disappear."

"Oh no," Esquire said, shaking her head.

"We'll need to isolate and question them individually, Esquire," Mr. Pepper said.

Alphonse flicked one of his earlobes. "I can hear the human patrol approaching. We need to get under cover soon. We should just make it to the villa in time. But let's put a move on."

"Why was Jewel next to her brother during the incident?" Mr. Pepper asked, huffing along to keep up with Esquire's quickened pace. "That certainly sounds suspicious."

"There's a good explanation. She's his dancer and backup singer." Alphonse paused. "Or she *was*."

"I always thought Beatle was a solo performer," Esquire said. "On all my albums, he's the only one on the cover."

"She's been backing him up the whole time," Alphonse said. "I don't think she made it onto any of the covers, though."

"An overlooked sister, always in the background. Interesting," Mr. Pepper said.

"She's not overlooked anymore," Alphonse said. "If the concert goes on as planned, she'd be the logical choice for the starring role."

"We appear to already have our prime suspect, Mr. Pepper," Esquire said as they hurried off toward the villa.

CHAPTER

The resort villa was a jumble of red-orange roofs, white stucco walls, and sun-bleached pool patios. Open-air corridors led here and there and everywhere, with wicker chairs at regular intervals so guests could relax and sip a coconut drink or read a magazine. All of it was overhung with palm trees whose trunks, Esquire couldn't help noticing, were the perfect distance from each other for stringing hammocks between. She did like a hammock. If they had been on a vacation after all, and not on a rescue mission. (Maybe someday someone would finally invite them on a simple social visit! Was that too much to ask?)

Humans were crawling over every surface as

humans will do, shouting at one another and scribbling on clipboards, preparing for the big Dizzy Dillinger concert. Esquire, Mr. Pepper, and Alphonse peered out from thick shrubbery while a roving patrolman clomped past. "Even if we succeed at avoiding the regular guard patrols, it's going to be very hard to travel around the villa without risking capture," Esquire reported from behind her binoculars.

"You're only a few dozen feet away," Mr. Pepper clucked. "You don't need those fool contraptions."

"Yes, I certainly do," Esquire sniffed. "Haven't you noticed how important I look while using them?"

"There will be even more humans once the party guests start to arrive," Alphonse said in his clicking bat voice. "We'll have to get our rescuing and sleuthing done before that happens."

"Let's begin with our prime suspect, then," Mr. Pepper said. "Jewel's room is . . . ?"

"Up at the top there," Alphonse finished, pointing dramatically with one of his wings while he used the other to hold up his key ring belt. "That's where all the exotic animals are kept."

Esquire whizzed her head round and saw a field of rough white stucco through the binoculars. "It looks impregnable. No doors or windows."

"That's because you're only seeing one brick," Mr. Pepper said, pecking the binoculars so they came away from Esquire's face.

"Ah," she said. "Whoopsie."

"Jewel's left the window open for us," Alphonse said. "I can get in easily, since no one cares where a bat goes. But a fox in a pink-and-green jacket would catch attention."

"It's true, a nice neutral linen would have been more appropriate for the Bahamas," Esquire said. "But don't you just love the green leaves on a pink background?"

"No human clothes at all would be the most appropriate," Mr. Pepper added, conveniently ignoring the strawberry apron still tied around his middle. "Now, Alphonse, what do you think about using the cabana roofs over the pool as a way to get to Jewel? We can get to the first one by climbing that nearby palm tree. Then, if we can hop between them, we'll reach the window. All above the usual human sight lines."

"Righto, Mr. Pepper!" Esquire said. "That's using the old bird brain."

Mr. Pepper was so outraged that his beak stuck wide open.

"Um, let's get this started!" Esquire said, manually closing Mr. Pepper's beak before clapping her paws. (Since they were paws, they didn't make any noise.)

Alphonse went first. As a bat, he didn't need a palm tree and cabana tents to scale the building. He simply zoomed up to the windowsill and waved his wings wildly. Esquire could see, because she was using her *binoculars*. "See, Mr. Pepper, it was a great idea after all that I brought—"

But Mr. Pepper was already on his way, toddling along the sand on his rooster legs until he was at the base of the palm tree. Esquire hurried to catch up to him, keeping an eye out for any human interest. As usual, they tended not to notice animals very much. Maybe they hadn't even realized that Beatle was missing. Hold on, Beatle, Esquire said to herself, we'll get you out of that hole as soon as possible!

"I don't think I'll be able to make it up this palm on my own," Mr. Pepper said, flexing his wings at the base of the tree.

"Good thing foxes are *very* good at climbing trees," Esquire said. She hid their duffel under a bush, tucked Mr. Pepper into her jacket, and scampered up. From the top of the palm, it was easy going over the cabana roofs to the wall. Humans were everywhere, but Esquire had long ago realized that although they often looked around them, they usually failed to look *up*. Now there were a good six feet of sheer vertical wall above them, though, and Esquire wasn't quite sure how to get up that. Foxes might be good at climbing, but not *that* good.

Alphonse called from the windowsill. "Hold on a second. I have an idea."

"Make it snappy!" Esquire said. A cluster of human voices was approaching from within the villa. She was totally exposed, her orange fur surrounded by the blazing white of the tent and wall. It would be only a matter of time before she was spotted.

She waited long moments, heart racing. Somewhere below, Dizzy Dillinger and his entourage approached.

Esquire couldn't see him, because she was crouched with her head under her forelegs, to make herself as small as possible. But she could hear him, singing one of his hits. "Oh, baby, you're the one for meeeeeeeee." He made that one last word into no fewer than eighteen different notes. Show-off.

"Dizzy, you sound great today! Yes, that's A. Maze. Ing. You're going to have the number one album again for sure," the employees around him said.

These humans clearly didn't know good music. Dizzy Dillinger's songs weren't Esquire's kind of thing. Beatle the Pangolin, however—*that* was true artistic genius!

Dizzy's voice trailed off. "Any of you seen Beatle around?" he asked his human companions. "Which one of you is supposed to take care of my pets on this trip?"

The entourage descended into chaotic chatter,

everyone accusing someone else. Esquire couldn't make many words out.

"Psst," came Alphonse's voice. "Up here, Esquire!"

The bat had reappeared at the windowsill above. Next to him was a face. It was long, with calm black eyes below a crest of shiny scales. It all ended in an adorable snub nose. "Hi there," she said, as that nose wiggled. "I'm Jewel. Thank you for answering my call for help."

"A pleasure," Esquire called up. "I do believe you're the first pangolin I've had the pleasure of rescuing."

"It seems more like she's rescuing us at the moment," Mr. Pepper corrected. "And I do hope we can hurry along with that part of all this."

Jewel cast down a length of shiny gold fabric. "It's a curtain cord from the suite. Go on, climb up!"

Esquire gave the tassel a good yank. It held fine. "Ready, Mr. Pepper?" she asked.

"Ready for the last climb I'll take in my life, you mean?" Mr. Pepper replied.

"I'll take that as a yes," Esquire said. She placed her back paws against the wall and then used the silken cord to haul herself up, pull by pull. It wasn't so hard, really! Now she could add mountaineering to her list of skills. Maybe.

As she neared the top, she whispered up to Jewel, "How did you get this to hold so steady?"

Jewel glanced away nervously, then opened her mouth to speak. But she didn't need to say anything, because Esquire had already reached the top, and as she dismounted she saw why the curtain cord was held so firmly.

It was in the mouth of a very large wildcat.

"Animal Rescue Agency, at your service," Esquire said, hiding her eyes behind her paws.

CHAPTER

Once it was clear that the wildcat wasn't going to eat her and Mr. Pepper, at least not right away, Esquire allowed herself a glance around.

Her first thought was that Dizzy's pets had it *made*. There was a faux-fur daybed for the wildcat, trimmed in fine purple silk. The monkey had a carved wooden tree to climb, painted in bright fuchsia and studded with rhinestones. Jewel had a pangolin-sized napping couch, covered in unbleached silk pillows that (Esquire couldn't help but notice) would look lovely in her own den. On the coffee table were bowls of fruit for the monkey, a terrarium full of crickets for Jewel, and the raw meat of some unfortunate creature for the wildcat.

There was also a copy of *Island Living* magazine that Esquire wouldn't mind getting her paws on.

It looked like everything these animals could want . . . but all the same, the door was solidly closed. Each pet had a collar and a tag. It might be a fancy one, but this hotel room was still a jail. Being a pet was weird that way.

"Who's this?" the wildcat asked as Esquire set down Mr. Pepper and straightened her pink-and-green jacket. The cat's eyes were only for the rooster. Cats had a tendency to be drawn to Mr. Pepper.

The rooster's feathers bristled, and he opened his beak to squawk but didn't get a sound out before Esquire interrupted. "I'm Esquire Fox and this is Mr. Pepper," she said, standing tall on her back legs so she could forcibly close Mr. Pepper's beak. "We're with the Animal Rescue Agency."

The exotic pets stared back at her. Esquire cleared her throat. "You . . . haven't heard of us?"

"It vaguely rings a bell," the monkey said as she scratched an armpit. She peered into Esquire's disappointed face. "We meet a *lot* of famous humans and animals around here. That doesn't mean we're not glad to meet you, sweet thing. I've never met anyone from a rescue agency before. Only talent agencies. I'm Arabella. The show director. I'm quite famous, too. It seems like everyone's famous these days, am I right?!"

"You said it," Jewel said. "We used to be special. Now 'celebrities' are a dime a dozen."

"We don't need you to think we're celebrities," Esquire said, suddenly emotional. "We don't do this for fame. . . ." Her voice trailed off. She was sounding pretty pathetic, she realized.

Mr. Pepper struggled free of her paw so he could squawk. "It's for the best that you don't know about us. We prefer to do our work in secrecy."

"That's right, Mr. Pepper, well said," Esquire said, nodding wildly. Then she couldn't resist adding: "Even if it would be nice to be invited to fancy parties every once in a while. As *guests*, I mean, instead of just rescuers." Mr. Pepper stared at her, shocked. Esquire stammered on. "I—I mean, not that there's anything wrong with being rescuers!"

The wildcat's tail thrashed. "You're rescue agents? Did you call in this meddling duo, Jewel?"

"Of course I did, Butch," Jewel said, cringing under the wildcat's intense gaze. "Why wouldn't I? My brother is missing!"

"We four were all equal parts of Dizzy's pet squad," Butch said. "At least I thought we were. But now it seems you've called in . . . independent representation."

"I assure you, we are not here to choose sides. Only to rescue Beatle," Esquire said. "Isn't that right, Mr. Pepper?"

Mr. Pepper was still too worked up to squawk out any words. That was probably for the best.

Esquire rushed on. "So. Let's start at the beginning. Our first priority is to save that pangolin. Who has ideas on how to rescue Beatle? Or has info on how this accident occurred in the first place?"

Arabella flounced down from her painted tree and collapsed on the floor, flinging one arm across her eyes dramatically. "I know you must be suspicious of me, since I direct the show and it's the platform that failed. But I swear it was working, and it was all Beatle's idea in the first place! We've tried everything to get him out of the crevasse: holding out a rope, singing to him.

Nothing works. We even lowered a bucket for him to get into, but it's far too tight down there." She pounded her little monkey fists against the carpet.

Esquire shuddered, thinking of what it would be like to be wedged in a crevasse in the dark. Although many pangolins slept in underground burrows, so maybe it wasn't *so* horrifying for Beatle. "Have any animals gone down there to investigate?"

The exotic pets shook their heads.

Esquire cast a glance to Alphonse, who nodded. A bat would be a natural choice to explore a narrow crevasse. She turned back to Arabella. "We're heading directly to the accident site after this, to see what we can manage for Beatle," she said. She drew herself up to her full height and clasped her paws behind her back. "But before I go, it's my duty to inform you that all three of you are suspects. I'd like to hear exactly where each of you were on the night Beatle went missing."

"See?" Butch growled. "This *is* an investigation!"

"Why, that's too easy to answer!" Arabella exclaimed, bounding from the floor and scratching the other armpit. "We were all at the animal concert venue, near the cliff at the far side of the villa. There are no roads going there, so we can be certain that no humans are around, as long as we're done and out of there before the two-hour guard patrols come around."

"She's right; we were all there. Arabella chose the location," Jewel added quietly. "And Butch was on guard."

"And you, madame?" Mr. Pepper asked. "Where were you the moment that Beatle disappeared?"

"That's your name, Butch?" Esquire asked the wildcat simultaneously. "Sorry, Mr. Pepper, you go first."

"No, no, go ahead," Mr. Pepper said.

Butch extended and retracted a claw before smoothing it over his hair. Mr. Pepper gave a squawk of alarm.

Esquire rolled her eyes at the obvious attempt at intimidation. Cats. "And what's your role in the production, Butch?"

"Hanger-on," Butch said sarcastically.

"Butch is a beloved member of the pet squad," Jewel said. "But he doesn't have a strict role in the animal concerts. At least, not anymore."

Esquire was about to ask her precisely what she meant by that, when Butch interrupted. "Before you go any further with this unauthorized investigation," Butch said, "I think it's time we got real. The simplest explanation for why Beatle stopped responding to our calls is that he's dead. It's time we moved on from even discussing a rescue and instead started planning how we're going to handle the concert."

"*Handle the concert?*" Jewel squeaked, shocked. "How dare you? How can we even think about that, when my brother is missing!"

Esquire bit her lip. That's very unpleasant with teeth as sharp as hers, so she tried to avoid it in general. She had no idea if pangolins were good liars. She wished she could have started with a private conversation with Jewel, rather than be thrust into this group lineup. All the same, being the world's top animal rescue agent demanded flexibility. Even when the animals she was working with didn't recognize her fame or invite her to parties, duty called. She would have to carry on.

She gave a glance to Mr. Pepper, to see if he had anything to contribute. He was still stuck with his beak half-open, feathers aquiver. "How do you propose that the concert would go on?" Esquire asked Butch.

"Animals are traveling here from far and wide to come to this show, and it would be terrible to disappoint them. If Jewel is too distraught, and Arabella is needed to direct the production . . ." Butch let his words trail off and started cleaning his paws again—which just happened to reveal his long sharp claws.

"You?" Jewel asked haughtily. "Animals haven't traveled across the world to hear a cat sing. No animal in history has ever *wanted* to hear a *cat* sing."

Esquire looked at her in surprise. This was a new side of Jewel. It seemed favored-pet status came with some snobbery included. "I think we're getting ahead of ourselves," Esquire said hastily. "Let's all take a breath and remember our primary goal: recovering Beatle."

"Like I said—" Butch started.

"He's down there!" Jewel said hotly. "We just have to get him out!"

Mr. Pepper finally found the wherewithal to squawk. "I am *not* cat food, Mr. Wildcat!"

Jewel burst into tears, and while Arabella comforted her, Esquire stared into her paws. She was at a complete loss. She'd proved once again that group negotiation was not her strong suit. What *was* her strong suit? This mission was making her feel a little insecure.

"Perhaps a quick team huddle is in order?" Mr. Pepper asked Esquire and Alphonse.

"Good idea," said the bat.

Esquire kneeled on the rug so that the three of them—fox, rooster, and bat—could look one another in the eyes. "Any thoughts?" she whispered.

"Clearly something underhanded is going on," Mr. Pepper said. "With an evident main suspect."

"Yes, it's clearly Jewel," Alphonse whispered.

"No, I think it's Butch," Mr. Pepper huffed.

"I had my eye on Arabella, actually," Esquire said.

They stared at one another in shock. "Okay, fine," Esquire said. "We'll need to clear two suspects, and then we'll be left with the culprit. We'll start by clearing Jewel."

"Fine," Mr. Pepper whispered. "Even though the villain is clearly Butch."

"Jewel," Alphonse said.

"Arabella," said Esquire.

Oh dear.

A long silence ticked by in the pet room. Mr. Pepper kept his eye trained on Butch, Butch stared back at Mr. Pepper, Arabella groomed her foot hair for parasites, and Jewel sobbed noisily into her pangolin claws. Alphonse perched on the windowsill and rubbed his wings together, pausing once in a while to adjust his key ring belt whenever it dropped around his ankles.

Esquire kept running through her mental list of suspects. Monkey, wildcat, pangolin. Monkey, wildcat, pangolin. It was so much to think about that she didn't have any thoughts left over to come up with anything to say.

So no one spoke. No one spoke for a long time.

It was awkward. It was very awkward.

This sleuthing business was not Esquire's favorite. She much preferred straightforward rescuing.

But there *was* a rescue to be done! Esquire clapped her paws. "Jewel, let's get Beatle back. Would you take me to where your brother was last seen?"

"Oh, sure. Of course you'd slink off together," Butch scoffed.

Arabella shook her finger at the wildcat. "We can't all go; then the humans would notice Dizzy's pets were missing and get suspicious. Jewel and the rescue agents should go. That's fine by me. I have no information to add anyway—I'm as surprised as anyone by Beatle's disappearance," Arabella said. She'd somehow managed to start grooming both armpits at once, which made her look quite ridiculous.

"Let's get going," Esquire said to Jewel. "We can talk along the way."

"I'll stand guard here and make sure none of these suspects gets up to any shenanigans," Mr. Pepper clucked.

"I don't think leaving you here is such a good idea," Esquire said, looking at the wildcat.

"He'll be fine," Arabella said. "Butch wouldn't dare get up to anything. I'm here to help stand guard."

Esquire cut a glance to Alphonse. "We need you with us," Esquire said. "You're going to be our scout."

Alphonse nodded, bat ears wobbling. "I'll tell Beatle you're on the way. Meet you there!" He bowed, hitched up his key ring belt one last time, and soared out the window.

Sniffling tearfully all the while, Jewel climbed her slow and steady pangolin way up a curtain tassel, then dropped out of view. "Thank you for holding down the fort, Mr. Pepper," Esquire said before scampering after. She had no doubt he'd be fine. He'd come out on top time and again after many carnivore confrontations—including his first meeting with Esquire herself!

Esquire felt her fur warm up right away once she was out under the brilliant sun. Jewel confidently brought them up the wall and over the roof of the villa, before stretching to grasp a branch and climb down to the sand. Esquire huffed to catch up—Jewel was very agile for a pampered pet! They passed between humps of low grass and dunes, crossing over the rubbery roots of palms, until the greenery gave way to sand. There was more and more sound of surf as Esquire and Jewel approached a desolate rocky cliff.

Esquire lowered her nose to the volcanic rock. She could still pick up the lingering fragrance of the roadies: the iguanas (not delicious) and the hutias (very delicious). There was also the scent of a pangolin, this one with a slightly different odor from Jewel's. It had a chemical tang to it. "Was Beatle wearing . . . fresh nail polish?" Esquire asked, nose wriggling.

Jewel had been staring sadly out to sea and then looked at Esquire, startled. "Yes, I'd just helped apply it. How did you know?"

Esquire tapped her nose. "Foxes are pretty good at the whole scent thing."

"So are pangolins," Jewel said. "I bet you can't distinguish between dozens of ant species with yours."

"No, and thank goodness. Why would I ever want to do that?" Esquire lowered her nose again and tracked the scent to the middle of the clifftop—where, sure enough, there was a big hole. "This crevasse is where the stage was?"

"Yes," Jewel said. "It had been positioned right on top. You can still see some of the holes where the crew had screwed in supports. They do a good job for hired hands." Her eyes filled up with tears again. "At least they usually do!"

Esquire paced the stage area and then looked into the split in the rocks. The light went only a short way before the hole was pure darkness. "Hello down there!" she called, paws around her snout to make a sort of megaphone.

"I'm down here!" came Alphonse's little voice. "I'll be up in a second."

"Okay!" Esquire called. Other than the bat, there were no sounds she could detect in the crevasse, even with her sensitive fox ears. She could tell from the echo of Alphonse's voice that the crevasse went very deep indeed. There couldn't be much food down there. Even if Beatle was okay for now, he wouldn't be for long. "Have you sent water and food down?" she asked Jewel.

She nodded and nudged a nearby rope with her nose. "Every few hours we send down water and a bundle of ants that I pick out myself. Only Beatle's favorite species."

"Excellent," Esquire said. "That will keep his morale up. Good thinking."

Jewel shook her head sadly. "When we pull the rope back up, the food and water are still there. He must be too far down to reach. Or else . . . he's passed out, maybe?"

Passed out . . . or worse. Esquire stared into the blackness, listening to the sounds of crashing waves while she waited for Alphonse to return.

"Should we—" Jewel started to say. But she was interrupted by the bat arrowing up out of the crevasse and into the sky.

Alphonse plopped to the ground before them. "I couldn't get deep enough to see him, but I managed to talk to him. Beatle is still alive! He has a message for his sister."

"Thank goodness!" Jewel said, bursting into tears again.

"I think I can go even farther and reach him, now that I've done so much echolocating around the underground system," Alphonse said. With that, he took a step toward the crevasse.

"No, wait!" Esquire cried. "Before you go, you have to tell us what Beatle said!"

"Oh, right," Alphonse replied. "Sorry. I memorized his words and everything." The bat cleared his throat and turned to face Jewel.

CHAPTER

"Would you like me to leave," Esquire asked Jewel, "so that you can hear what your brother had to say to you in private?"

Jewel shook her head. "No. I like having you here. I'm a little scared about what I'm about to hear, to tell you the truth," Jewel said.

"Whatever it is, it's better to know than to sit around worrying," Esquire said gently.

"Yes," Jewel said tearfully, kneading her claws. "I suppose you're right."

"Would you two hurry up?" Alphonse asked. "I don't want to forget what he said before I've had a chance to tell it. We bats don't have the best memory."

Jewel took a deep breath. She nodded.

Alphonse crossed a wing before him theatrically and gave a little bat cough before doing some trilling vocal warm-ups. "Okay, here goes. 'I just want to say goodbye, sister. I'm sorry I won't be able to live up to everyone's expectations of me. If I'm unable to get out, please give all my starring roles to . . .'" Alphonse's voice trailed off.

"That's *it*?" Esquire asked. "He didn't finish?"

"No, he finished," Alphonse said, a wounded expression on his face as he dabbed his brow. "I just needed to check my memory. This speech was long. Okay, here I go."

He reassumed his theatrical position, wing drawn in front like a bullfighter's cape. Then he scratched his head. "Where was I?"

"'If I'm unable to get out, please give all my starring roles to . . .'" Esquire prompted.

"Oh, right! 'If I'm unable to get out, please give all my starring roles to my beloved little sister, Jewel. But I'd prefer to come out of this hole alive, obviously.'"

Alphonse looked between them expectantly, like he was waiting for them to erupt into applause.

He'd have to wait for a while. Esquire didn't know a pangolin could look pale, but Jewel had gone practically see-through.

"That can't be right," she said. Jewel's narrow little pangolin nose was trembling. She leaned over the crevasse. "You never asked me about this! I don't want to be a world-famous star! I just want my brother!" she wailed.

Everyone was being so very dramatic. Must come with the pampered-pet territory. Esquire tugged Jewel away from the edge, worried she might wind up with two pangolins down that crevasse instead of just one. She gave the grieving pangolin the tightest hug she could give. "We can send Alphonse down with a reply," Esquire whispered. "What would you like to tell your brother?"

Jewel took a deep breath, then removed herself from Esquire's hug. She leaned low over the ground, so she could look into Alphonse's eyes. "Thank you for getting this message to my brother," she said.

Alphonse nodded solemnly, wing fingers resting on his key ring belt.

"Tell him that I don't accept. That we'll be getting him out from that hole, whether he likes it or not. He's my brother, and I'm not losing him."

Esquire nodded. "He's not alone, Alphonse. Make sure he knows that we won't rest until he's free."

The bat nodded and saluted. Then he scratched his head. "Don't you want to hear the rest of what he had to say before I go back down, though?"

"What? There's more?" Esquire exclaimed. "Why didn't you say so?"

"You were having your tender moment," Alphonse sniffed. "I didn't want to intrude."

"What is it?" Jewel asked. "What did my brother say?"

Alphonse cleared his throat and brought himself up to his full (though minimal) height. "He said 'Butch. Butch is the one who—'"

Alphonse's ears flicked. "Someone's coming! The human patrol! Hide!"

Esquire and Jewel bolted for the bushes, while Alphonse scrambled off the edge and dropped into the chasm.

CHAPTER

7

They had no time to discuss that strange half news, not when they were running for their lives!

The nearest cover was a good twenty feet away along the rocky cliff, and Esquire was just able to get under the salt-crusted branches of a low pine bush when she heard the heavy steps of the approaching guard. She pressed her body low and looked back . . . to see that Jewel had made it only halfway across the clearing. Pangolins were not the fastest.

"Hurry up," Esquire hissed, then had to break off,

because the human had come within earshot. She caught her breath as she watched the black boots clump across the rock toward the pangolin, trapped out in the open.

The patrol! Forgot to plan for that one. The human slowed. "What's this?"

When Esquire looked at Jewel, she saw that the pangolin had rolled herself up into a lumpy sort of pear. Her face and claws were hidden, so she was simply a ball of scales. She looked a lot like—

"What an unusual pine cone!" the guard said, squatting down to get a better look. "My kids would like this for their arts and crafts box." He reached forward for the pine cone . . . and it rolled a foot away.

"That's a weird pine cone. Come here, pine cone."
He reached for it again . . . and it rolled away again.

"The weirdest pine cone I've ever seen." The guard crept over, sighing . . . and the pine cone rolled right into the pine bush.

He paused, gulped, and then clomped away, muttering about having done too much overtime.

. . . at which point the pine cone unrolled at Esquire's paws, becoming Jewel again.

"Wow," Esquire said. "Nice trick!"

"Thanks," Jewel said distractedly. "Now let's go let everyone know what my brother said about Butch."

"Only problem is that we don't exactly know what he said about Butch," Esquire said. "Alphonse got cut off." She leaned over the crevasse. "Alphonse, come back!"

There was no answer.

"I think we should go," Jewel said. "Alphonse will catch up. I don't want to leave Butch unsupervised right now."

"Agreed," Esquire said. "Alphonse will let Beatle know we'll be back, but for now I especially don't want Mr. Pepper to be around that wildcat."

Without another word, they raced through the underbrush and scampered back up the wall toward the exotic pets.

Esquire paused at the top of the curtain tassel that lead into the room. "Let's not go accusing Butch right away," she whispered. "We have more advantage if he doesn't know what we know."

"My thoughts exactly," Jewel whispered. "Especially since we don't know precisely why Beatle said Butch's name."

They dropped in.

Esquire had thought that the worst part of all this would be telling everyone that she'd been unable to rescue Beatle. But no, the worst part would be telling a jealous monkey and wildcat about Beatle's unexpected plans for his sister to take his place in his concert.

"That does sound like something Beatle would do," Arabella said once Jewel had shared the news, worrying her claws together where she sat on the middle of the coffee table. "You know, making a huge life choice that affects us all dramatically and not including any of us in the planning."

"This is rich, is what I think," Butch growled at Esquire. "You expect us to believe that you wander out into the human world in your perfectly tailored jacket and within a few minutes your agent has found out that your client is now a celebrity, just like that? Neither of you heard this directly from Beatle, did you? This all sounds like some trick."

Esquire startled. It did all look a little suspicious, now that Butch had put it that way. She was feeling hot under her fur. It was especially bothersome to be accused by their new number one suspect. At least he liked her jacket. "There's no reason for anyone to go accusing anyone," Esquire said. "The best defense is a good offense, as they say. It's almost like you know *you* have something to hide." She jabbed her forepaw in the air, feeling very much like a real detective as she did. "Make a note of all this, Mr. Pepper!"

"What are you talking about?" Mr. Pepper said. He raised one of his scaled feet. "I can't take notes with these!"

"We just have to get Beatle out of there," Jewel said. "Nothing else matters."

"You're right about that much," Butch said, looking at Jewel shrewdly.

Arabella scratched an armpit. "It's not for us to decide whether your brother was being logical. We still need to honor his wishes. You should go on for him on Saturday, dear. And yes, in the meantime let's do everything we can to get him free."

Butch whirled to face the monkey. "This arrangement will also allow you to still direct a show, won't it?

All you've done is swap one pangolin for another—one that's more open to your direction!"

"What are you accusing me of?" Arabella squeaked, nearly fainting. "Are you claiming that *I* sabotaged Beatle's stage? Moi?!"

"Make notes of this, Mr. Pepper!" Esquire said out of the side of her mouth.

"I told you, I can't write with chicken claws!" he clucked back.

"All I'm saying," Butch growled, "is that something fishy is going on. Beatle's trapped away, and you two are thrust into the spotlight, while I'm cut out entirely."

"Are you really making my brother's tragedy all about *you*?" Jewel asked, raising her tearstained face from her hands.

"Butch is right about one thing. I'm a terrific judge of character, and this is just so unlike Beatle, to give away his starring role," Arabella said. "He loved the spotlight. He loved it more than any of us. He's basically Dizzy Dillinger, only in a pangolin body."

"Yes," Butch said, his eyes glittering as he stared at Jewel. "No one else could shine in the spotlight while he was around."

"That's right," Jewel said, her eyes glittering right

back. "None of us could. Some of us were more comfortable with that fact than others. Isn't that true, Butch?"

"I do hope you're getting all this, Mr. Pepper," Esquire whispered. He squawked in frustration.

"You put on a good act, little sister," Butch said, hackles rising.

"*I* put on a good act?" Jewel asked hotly, putting her face right in the wildcat's.

Jewel was about to give away what they'd learned from Alphonse! Esquire put herself right in Butch's face. "Hold it right there, Butch. I don't care one lick who's a star and who's not. We have a pangolin to rescue. That's the only thing that matters."

Butch bared his long teeth. "I refuse to take direction from a jacket-wearing fox!"

"What does everyone have against my jacket?!" Esquire yelled. "It makes me happy to wear it, and that's enough! Isn't that right, Mr. Pepper?"

"Well, erm, you know how I feel about all these human clothes you like to wear," Mr. Pepper said, fluffing his feathers and avoiding Esquire's gaze.

"*Mr. Pepper!* You're wearing a *strawberry apron!*"

"What's that noise?" Mr. Pepper said, pointing his beak at the door.

"Don't try to make up a distraction now, Mr. Pepper," Esquire said, her paw at her chest. "I'm very disappointed in you right now."

"No, he's right, *shh*," Jewel said.

Esquire held still. That's when she heard a melodious male human voice out in the hallway. "Beatle? Where are youuuu?" The voice repeated the line twice more, the words becoming indecipherable as he got distracted, experimenting with melodies.

"It's Dizzy!" Jewel hissed.

Arabella began running in a circle, long monkey arms flailing. "Go, go! Exit stage left, fox and rooster!"

Mr. Pepper had already hopped to the window. "We need to get out of here, Esquire. Now."

"We'll be back," Esquire said hastily as she lifted herself up to the windowsill. "Keep an eye on one another, okay?" She beamed a message to Jewel. *Watch out for Butch especially. We're off to save your brother.*

That's one advantage of the fact that Dizzy basically keeps his animals prisoner, Esquire thought as she followed the clucking rooster out the window and off into freedom: the three suspects are already in jail.

Now it was up to Esquire and Mr. Pepper to get Beatle out of the crevasse once and for all.

Even more humans were swarming about now, so Esquire and Mr. Pepper stayed as quiet as they could as they skulked through shadows and along rooftops.

It was the hardest silence Esquire had ever put herself through, because she was bursting with thoughts on how to rescue Beatle. Bursting!

As soon as they were out of the view of boots and heels, Esquire opened her mouth to start listing those thoughts.

They could recruit naked mole rats!

They could pour seawater into the crevasse until Beatle floated to the top!

They could build a huge ladder out of seashells! (She still had to think more about that last one.)

But Mr. Pepper fluffed his feathers, a sign that he wanted Esquire to shut right up. So she did.

"Do you feel that?" Mr. Pepper asked, inclining his head.

She felt the hot sun on her fur, but Mr. Pepper surely couldn't mean that. Then Esquire realized what he was referring to—the ground was trembling a little.

"Something is crumbling underground. The crevasse walls could drop debris on Beatle. We need to get him out as soon as possible."

Esquire consulted the pocket watch she kept in her jacket pocket. It hadn't worked for years, but just looking at the clock face helped her think about time issues. "If he's sticking to the two-hour schedule, the patrolling guard shouldn't be by for at least an hour yet, so let's act now."

With that, Mr. Pepper was off—and at surprising speed. It was actually great terrain for a chicken. Mr. Pepper had no problem ducking under bushes, and his clawed feet made short work through sand. Esquire was having a harder go of it. She had burrs between her paw pads, and the heat was making her light-headed. "Good thing we'll pass by the duffel we stashed away," she said. "I'm going to fish out my other beach sandals and my sun hat."

"Of course you're not," Mr. Pepper said. "We need to get to Beatle as fast as possible."

Esquire nodded. "Of course." She was going to go this entire trip without once getting to wear that sun hat; she was sure of it.

They'd reached the crevasse. Mr. Pepper leaned his head over the gap, the gentle updrafts ruffling his feathers. He looked at Esquire with searching eyes. "There's no sign of him."

"Yes," Esquire said slowly. Had Mr. Pepper's brain overheated? "Beatle's stuck deep in this crevasse. That's why we're here."

"Not *Beatle*," Mr. Pepper said crossly. "Alphonse!"

"Oh!" Esquire said, startled. "You're right! He should

be out by now." She cupped her paws around her snout. "Alphonse? Are you down there?" The sound of the ocean surf was the only reply, and Esquire's gut began to twist.

The twisting of her gut was really dramatic now, shaking even her paws. No, wait a second, that wasn't her gut—that was the crevasse, trembling again! "Back up," she ordered Mr. Pepper. Even her whiskers were vibrating.

Together, they pushed back from the crevasse's edge, Esquire protectively covering Mr. Pepper with her forelegs. The sand that dusted the rocky cliff trembled and popped in the air as the ground shook. Clods of dirt tumbled into the crevasse.

"It's going to cave in entirely!" Mr. Pepper squawked.

"Which would be the end of both Beatle and Alphonse," Esquire said. "I won't let that happen!" She wasn't sure *how* she wasn't going to let that happen, however.

Mr. Pepper bravely toddled to the crevasse and looked down. "Alphonse and Beatle, we're coming to save you," he cawed.

Esquire slunk to join him at the edge. Mr. Pepper fluffed up his underfeathers as he peered down. "I can hop to that ledge there, and then work my way along.

If I squawk loud enough, then I might be able to get a response, and we can find out where they are and how we can help."

"But Mr. Pepper, you can't fly."

"I most certainly can!" Mr. Pepper said. "I just need some help, that's all. While I'm down there, you need to find a fallen tree or something, so I can hop along it to get back out."

"A fallen tree?! Are you serious, Mr. Pepper?"

"Yes, I most certainly am," Mr. Pepper said. With that, he hopped into the hole.

Esquire shrieked, but then she saw that Mr. Pepper was right—there was a ledge not six feet down, wide enough for a chicken to walk along. Which was just what he was doing. "Alphonse!" Mr. Pepper called. "Beatle! The crevasse is crumbling!"

"Mr. Pepper, this is too dangerous," Esquire called down.

"I agree, which is why you need to find a fallen tree for me, ASAP!" Mr. Pepper replied, as he shuffled farther along his ledge. "Hellooooo!"

With an eye to the edge of the clearing to make sure the patrolling guard wasn't approaching—he wasn't yet, but he would be eventually!—Esquire headed into the trees, searching for something that could help her get her foolish but very brave friend back out of the crevasse.

"I can't believe he'd go down there without even clearing it with me first," she grumbled to herself. All the same, she was swelling with pride. Sometimes she and Mr. Pepper were more alike than even she knew.

Finally, she found something that should work. A fallen palm frond, brittle and brown. It was heavy, though. She could barely drag it along the hot stone of the clifftop.

She moved backward across the cliff, midday heat making waves in the air. She kept her mouth open, tongue lolling, to cool down a little. Even so, she was still feeling light-headed.

Esquire dropped the frond at the edge of the crevasse and peered down. "Mr. Pepper?"

All was black, and all was still. "Mr. Pepper?"

Then a white shape appeared. A rooster-sized shape! He was farther down than he'd said he would go. Esquire wasn't sure the frond would reach. "Hold on, Mr. Pepper," Esquire said. "I'm going to lower this branch down. You might have to hop up to it, though."

"Okay, thank you!" Mr. Pepper called.

"Do you have Beatle?"

"No, I'm afraid not. But I did hear from Alphonse.

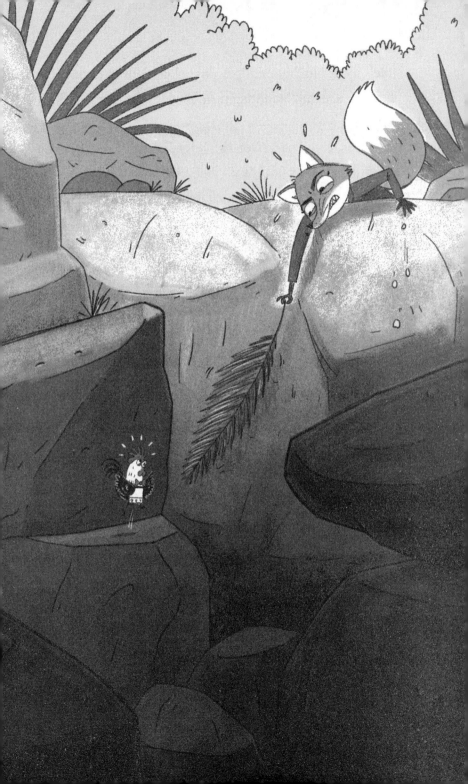

He's alive but trapped in a pocket by falling debris. He says he's heard sounds from Beatle, but they're both stuck!"

Esquire leaned over the edge, pushing the branch before her, fronds-down. "See this, Mr. Pepper?" she said, straining. "I'm going to lower it toward you, and I need you to hop onto the frond and then hop up and out of here, okay? Whoo, hurry up, this is heavy."

She lowered the awkward frond-y bit into the hole, then got a grip on the other end of the branch. As more and more entered the open space, though, it all got heavier and heavier. She gripped with all her might, finally lying on her side so she could hold on with her back paws, too. The frond was only getting heavier, and tipping into the crevasse faster!

"Mr. Pepper, hold on," she said through gritted teeth. "I'm . . . losing my grip here."

Then it was too much. The branch tipped over into the open space, and the back ripped through all four of Esquire's paws. It was dropping through the open air.

Esquire cried out. Not only would the branch be of no use for getting Mr. Pepper out of the crevasse, it might knock him deeper in!

For a split second, her heart ceased beating, her breath went still, and time stopped passing.

Until a shape streaked forward from behind Esquire and a paw gripped the branch, right before it fell entirely into the hole.

"Did I just do that?" Esquire said, looking at her own paws. But no, they were empty.

She whirled around to see Butch—Butch!—gripping the branch. Holding on to it was easy work for the muscular cat.

"What are you doing here?" Esquire said.

"No time for that," Butch hissed. "Look at the edge of the clearing."

Esquire saw the top of a familiar head. That animal-catching human. On patrol.

Oh no.

"Mr. Pepper, hurry!" Esquire said.

"Yes, good advice," Butch said dryly.

"Don't need to tell me twice," Mr. Pepper called. He jumped and fluttered his wings, landing midway up the branch, then hopped again so he was beside them on the cliff.

"So Alphonse . . ." Mr. Pepper started, trying to catch his breath.

"No time for that now," Butch hissed. "You need to get out of here."

Mr. Pepper saw the guard approaching. "Yes, we do."

"What's that there?" the guard called as he emerged from the cover of the palm trees. "Stop and reveal yourself!"

"It's okay if he sees me," Butch hissed. "*I'm* supposed to be on the island. But not a clothes-wearing fox and rooster."

Mr. Pepper squawked. "See, Esquire, I told—"

"Not now!" Esquire said. "Butch is right."

"Go into the bushes, over there," Butch said. "Now!"

Esquire and Mr. Pepper dashed for hiding. They could only hope they weren't too late.

CHAPTER

They *were* too late, because the moment Esquire and Mr. Pepper had made it into the brush and turned around, they saw the legs and feet of the human coming directly toward their hiding place. "Don't run, little guy. Dizzy is missing his precious pangolin!"

"Oh no, oh no," Esquire said as she and Mr. Pepper slunk farther back into the greenery. "He thinks he's found Beatle."

The feet drew ever closer. Dragging behind the man was a net. An animal-catching net.

Finally, the boots were right in front of the bush. Esquire bared her teeth and prepared to bite. They might be captured, but she would go down fighting.

The net disappeared from view. Because the man was preparing to use it. On them!

"Get ready to fight, Mr. Pepper," Esquire snarled. The rooster trembled beside her. Esquire held her forelegs out. Maybe the net would capture just her, and Mr. Pepper would have a chance to make a run for it.

The net never came, though, because a terrible caterwauling began on the far side of the clifftop.

The boots turned. Esquire bent back a branch to see what was making the noise.

It was Butch! And what a performance, too! His rhinestone collar glittered magnificently in the sun as he wailed. It was the worst kind of tomcat howling, with some extra spitting and snarling thrown in for good measure.

As the man approached, Butch changed tactics. He got up unsteadily to all fours, then hunched his shoulders and make hacking noises. A wonderful interpretation of dredging up a particularly sticky hair ball.

"Butch, I didn't even realize *you* were missing!" the human said.

Butch continued pretending to spit up his hair ball. *Hack. Glorp. Brach!*

"Oh, you don't look so good at all. Hold on, I'm going to pick you up, okay?"

Back arched, hair sticking up, Butch looked just like the cat decoration on a Halloween card. He didn't look like something that anyone in their right mind would want to be picking up. But then Butch laid his ears down and gave a pathetic mewling sound.

"Aww, it's okay, we'll get you all fixed up and feeling

better," the animal catcher said, kneeling down and scooping up Butch.

"That was a very convincing performance," Esquire whispered. "Worth noting what a good actor Butch is."

"Oh, I definitely noticed," Mr. Pepper replied. "I was just about to suggest we cross him off our suspect list, but now I'm not so sure."

The guard turned his back to them as he walked back toward the villa. Butch was draped over his shoulder, so they had a perfect view of the wildcat as he gave them a big, long-lashed wink.

"He did just save us from getting captured," Esquire said, tapping her chin with her paw as she picked her way out of the bush and brushed leaves from her linen jacket. "I'm not sure where this puts us, if he's more of a suspect or less of one. Never fear. We'll figure it out, my poultry friend."

"Harrumph," Mr. Pepper said as he smoothed his feathers back down. "I know you're in a good mood now that we've escaped capture, but that will be enough poultry talk."

"Whatever you say, my five-piece meal," Esquire said cheerfully.

Mr. Pepper sputtered in outrage. Esquire watched Butch as the guard carried him farther and farther away. The winking expression on his face was gone. It was replaced by something more sinister. The wildcat had a look of utter concentration on his features as he reached up a claw to unclip his rhinestone collar and dangle it over the crevasse. Even from across the clearing, Esquire could see that there was some sort of bundle attached to it.

She had a perfect view but was powerless to do anything as the cat dropped the collar—and its bundle—into the crevasse.

CHAPTER

10

"What in the world was that?" Mr. Pepper asked, cock-a-doodling despite himself.

"Keep it down, Mr. Pepper!" Esquire said, placing a paw over her friend's beak even as she squinted, trying to see if anything was happening to the crevasse, if it was erupting or exploding or anything.

Just like that, Butch was back to being a prime suspect. Maybe he'd attempted to murder Beatle the night of the dress rehearsal and now, having found out that Beatle was alive, he'd returned to finish the task!

Mr. Pepper clearly had the same train of thought. "I'm not as fast as you. I'll stay here and work on rescuing Beatle and Alphonse. You follow Butch, go!" he clucked.

It could be anything that Butch dropped into the crevasse—maybe a threatening note, maybe poison or explosives! Maybe this is why the crevasse had started crumbling in hours ago, through some other sabotage Butch had done.

Teeth bared, Esquire dashed out from the bush and stalked after the guard.

As she arrowed through the night, whipping around palm trees and through beach scrub, she glanced back at the crevasse and caught sight of Mr. Pepper, who was pacing the edge.

Esquire's heart raced. Very few animals were better at giving chase than a fox, and the human was doing nothing to cover his tracks. She'd be able to follow the catcher, no doubt—but what would she do once she'd found him? If it came to a fight, she'd be ready. A wildcat would be an even match for a fox, but she could take him. If she could get the human out of the way first.

The guard carried Butch upstairs, his boots visible through the drainage holes in the exterior stairwell as he clumped to the third floor. Esquire scrambled up a vertical storm drain, gripping the metal with all fours, making rending and scratching sounds as her claws dug into the painted aluminum.

With her sensitive fox ears, she detected the key rattling in the second door along the hallway. Rather than confront Butch there, while he was being held by the human, Esquire took to the exterior wall, working her way along the ledges to the second window.

A billowing curtain blocked her view. Esquire would have to drop in blind. It wasn't the safest move, but Esquire wasn't about to let her prime suspect slip away, no chance! She leaped into the room.

Esquire crouched as soon as she hit the carpet, teeth bared and claws extended. But no attack came. She scented Butch in the far corner of the room, unmoving. It took a few moments for Esquire's vision to adjust to the light. Once it did, she gasped.

This must be Dizzy Dillinger's room!

It was very fancy. Marble tabletops, a canopy bed with a linen topper, a minifridge with five different kinds of sparkling water visible through the frosted glass door, handsome two-tone luggage set in one corner, a music stand next to a TV that was as wide as

Esquire's entire den. None of it was a look she would aspire to in her own decorating, but it was impressive nonetheless.

Esquire placed one paw on the carpet, and then another. Approaching Butch. Her whole body was tensed in case he leaped into motion. But he remained motionless.

"Butch. What were you doing at the scene of the accident?" Esquire hissed. "Or should I say, 'the scene of the crime'?"

"Why should I tell you anything?" Butch hissed back. "You wouldn't believe me anyway. You've been determined to hate me from the start. Even after I saved you."

"That's simply not true," Esquire said. Now that she thought about it, though, it was maybe a little true. He was a mean wildcat named Butch, after all. Could he really be surprised that he was a suspect? "Tell me what you put down the crevasse just now."

"No." Butch lay in the corner, belly to the carpet, tail thrashing.

Clearly Esquire would need to take a more subtle route. Get into Butch's confidences. "Is this Dizzy Dillinger's suite?" she asked, getting up onto her back paws. She kicked them into her sandals, which had fallen off when she went down to all fours.

"Yes, it is," Butch said, a note of pride entering his voice as he stretched, stood, and paced along the carpet.

"It's very nice," Esquire said. "You must enjoy living in such luxury."

Butch didn't say anything in return. While Esquire was inspecting the walnut nightstand, the wildcat did something surprising. He stretched up to the doorknob and, with one smooth gesture, slid the dead bolt shut with his paw.

Esquire was too surprised to do anything to interrupt. "What is that for?" she asked, eyes narrowing.

"It's to prevent Dizzy from coming in and discovering you," Butch said.

"It also prevents me from *leaving* that way," Esquire pointed out, her claws extending on instinct. She was glad Mr. Pepper wasn't here, not if this was going to come to an out-and-out fight.

"Nothing to worry about," Butch purred. "I just don't want anyone to spot you in here. That might lead to some hard questions, don't you think?"

Esquire considered what to say next. This did feel like a prison. A very nicely decorated one, but still. At least the window was open.

"I noticed you admiring the bedside table," Butch said, licking a paw before running it through his silky hair. "Dizzy brings all the furnishings with him, wherever he goes. So that each tour stop feels like home."

"That sounds . . . expensive," Esquire said.

"Yes, very," Butch said proudly. The wildcat was becoming positively chatty. Esquire realized that he was probably lonely. Especially with Beatle gone.

"Do you get some say in how he chooses all the decorations?" Esquire asked politely, her front paws behind her back, like a human visiting a museum. Her heart was racing, but she tried not to let it show.

Her eye went to the window, judging how quickly she could make an escape. That was when she saw feathers.

There on the window ledge, half-hidden, was Mr. Pepper. He placed a wing over his beak. *Shh.*

Mr. Pepper must not have come up with anything to help Beatle. Or he'd gotten worried about Esquire's safety and followed her. Either way, Esquire was glad to have backup.

The truth was, even with Mr. Pepper nearby again, Esquire didn't feel fine about her situation. But the best way out that she could see was to ingratiate themselves with Butch, not to make him even more of an enemy.

He was the prime suspect in her mind, and maybe she could get him to trip up. Or she could find out what he had planned for her. She was confident she could handle whatever it was.

Soft clucks. Mr. Pepper's meaning was unmistakable: *Get out. Now.*

Of course Mr. Pepper would be less relaxed about the situation. He was a *chicken*. Chickens were famously delicious. If only Esquire could communicate with him in secret. As it was, all she could do was give him a meaningful look: *This is all a plan to get into Butch's confidences. Please understand!* She positioned herself so her head blocked Mr. Pepper from Butch's view.

"Would you like to see the closet?" Butch asked. "Dizzy has a whole set of shelves and racks dedicated to custom animal clothing. Some of it would fit you. Nothing that would look good on that old bird of yours, though."

"Oh!" Esquire said. "I'd love to see some custom animal clothing. I wonder if he has anything with rhinestones, like your collar. Where is your collar, by the way?"

No answer from Butch. An indignant cluck came from the direction of the window.

Esquire tried to send Mr. Pepper another meaningful look, but the rooster was clearly too incensed to notice any subtleties coming from her. That was a complicated look to pull off, anyway. Best she could do was slink after Butch into the walk-in closet.

Oh, wow. She knew she couldn't get distracted from her goal of rescuing Beatle, but this really was a clothes-wearing animal's dream. Esquire's gaze skipped all over the racks, trying to take everything in. All sorts of shoes, from tiny parrot flip-flops to sturdy steel-toed donkey boots. Pink lace gloves, perfectly sized for monkey hands. What appeared to be a penguin trench coat, complete with embroidered flipper holes. Esquire's eyes were drawn to a burgundy evening gown. Too impractical for her to wear, and clearly designed for an animal without a tail, so the back would look ridiculous. Still, it would be nice to try it on. Gowns weren't really her thing, but the fabric looked like it would feel pleasant as it slid over her fur.

You're here to get into Butch's confidences, not to go shopping, Esquire told herself sternly. (Her mind's voice sounded like Mr. Pepper's whenever she talked to herself sternly.)

"This is all very nice. You're such a lucky animal to

get to live and travel with Dizzy Dillinger," she said.

"I don't know about that," Butch said, his words trailing off. He settled into cleaning himself, which is a trick cats often do when they want to avoid a conversation.

Butch had conspicuously stopped in front of a poster of Dizzy, from one of his concert tours. He was a skinny teenaged human, blow-dried hair crushed down by a black baseball hat. He had many silver chains around his neck. It all seemed like a whole lot of pretending. Esquire knew that in animals showiness was often a sign of insecurity, but who knew how human minds worked.

"I didn't know Dizzy had any birds," Esquire said, taking up the parrot flip-flops and examining the craftsmanship. They had adorable little cowrie shells stitched into the thong and would look great on Mr. Pepper. She stole a glance at him. He was hopping up and down on the window ledge, clearly infuriated that Esquire hadn't yet beaten a retreat.

"He's had a long history of exotic pets," Butch said. "I think all the birds were from before my time."

"I wonder what happened to them," Esquire said casually. At least she meant to sound casual. Her heart started beating even faster when Butch didn't answer. He just stared at her, his eyes glittering. The poster of Dizzy in the background stared at her, too. His eyes were empty.

Esquire decided she didn't like this place at all. She had thought fame must be something wonderful, getting VIP invites to private island parties and all that, but she was learning that maybe it . . . wasn't?

She could sense the disappointment positively radiating off Mr. Pepper while she admired her way through the garments. "Oh, there's jewelry, too!"

As she and Butch leaned over a glass case of necklaces, broaches, and earrings, all of Esquire's thoughts were on her friend. *Please understand, Mr. Pepper!* Finally, she allowed herself to look over. He'd turned around, facing out into the night sky. Too disgusted to even look at her, no doubt.

Butch carefully lifted a glass lid with a claw, the hard nail making a high-pitched grinding noise that made Esquire cover her sensitive ears. He pulled out a diamond-studded collar and placed it around his neck. "Nice, right? I wear this on special occasions."

Esquire nodded. "It's lovely. Sets off your eyes beautifully." An inspiration struck her. "It makes you look almost as striking as Beatle, with all his rainbow polish."

One of Butch's ears cocked as he backed out of the closet and into the main room. "Thank you, I guess?"

"It must have been hard, what with Beatle getting so much attention all the time. I don't know how you put up with it," Esquire pushed.

"This is not your strong suit. You should stick to rescuing, not interrogating," Butch said.

"Then stop making me!" Esquire replied, digging her front paws into the pockets of her jacket. "Just tell me what you were doing out at the accident site. And maybe, I don't know, *help me rescue Beatle*!"

Butch paused. "I'm sworn to secrecy."

"Who swore you to secrecy?"

"I can't tell you."

"That's too bad, because I'm not letting you out of my sight until you *do* tell me."

Butch's ears went back. "Because I'm a suspect?"

"Of *course* you're a suspect," Esquire said. "That shouldn't be any surprise, should it?"

"No," Butch meowed, his tail twitching. "I guess not."

Esquire laid a tentative paw on Butch's hackles.

"Come on, just tell me exactly what's going on, so you don't have to sit with any secrets anymore. Won't it be nice to get everything off your chest?"

Butch closed his eyes. "It would be nice not to have to keep this a secret anymore."

Esquire caught Mr. Pepper's eyes. The rooster was expressionless. Esquire desperately tried to beam her intentions to him. Normally they could communicate volumes with a look, but they were not communicating so well these days. They'd been so peaceful and happy at home, and that all changed when they got around these animal celebrities. It was mostly Esquire's fault, she was sure, with her obsession with glamour and her hopes that this would be a party vacation. She could be vain and silly, she knew. If only she could get a chance to apologize.

Butch was close to confessing; Esquire was sure of it. Just a little nudge more, and she'd have the answers to everything. She decided to make one last attempt at worming her way into his good graces. "Do you think I could try on that collar? It really is beautiful."

There was an outraged cluck from the windowsill. Mr. Pepper had given up on her. He hopped off and disappeared.

Esquire dashed to the window in time to catch sight

of Mr. Pepper flapping his wings, slowing his fall, until he landed on the canvas tent over the pool and bounced off and out of view.

He'd abandoned her.

Esquire hesitated, undecided. Mr. Pepper was using this chance to make an escape. He probably expected Esquire to do the same. But if she escaped now, she'd lose her chance to get answers.

What to do?

She'd do her duty to the Animal Rescue Agency is what she'd do. She could make Mr. Pepper under-stand later.

And so she eased away from the win-dowsill and, heart quaking, padded toward Butch.

Or at least where she remembered Butch being. He wasn't there anymore. "Where'd you go?" Esquire called.

Then there was a noise—from behind her! Esquire whirled to face the windowsill, just in time to see Butch swipe the shutter closed with a paw. There was a click as it locked over the window.

Now Esquire truly was trapped.

Mr. Pepper couldn't remember exactly when he'd last been away from Esquire. But he remembered this feeling: Even though he thought he was full of frustration with her, only a few seconds after he was away from Esquire—pop—it was all gone and he missed her. That was the only feeling that remained. Missing Esquire.

That fool fox, Mr. Pepper thought as he bounced off the canvas pool awning. She was always letting herself get sidetracked. They were on a mission, an important mission. A pangolin was *trapped*, Alphonse was *missing*, they hadn't even begun to investigate Arabella, and there Esquire was preening through Dizzy's closet, oohing and aahing, as wide-eyed as a hen who'd laid a blue egg.

Mr. Pepper hit the ground on his fluff and bounced again. Bouncing, even from a great height, never really hurt a chicken—bird bones had lots of bend. It was hard to *stop* the bouncing, though. Once he'd rolled to a stop, Mr. Pepper positioned himself below the exotic pets' window. If Esquire was going to let Jewel and Beatle down, Mr. Pepper would have to work the case on his own. He could rescue Beatle from his collapsing crevasse, even without any help from that brainless fox.

Whom he missed.

He really hoped Esquire wasn't getting herself into real trouble up there.

Mr. Pepper had examined the crevasse as best as he could after Butch dropped his bundle down it. He'd paced the edge, calling for Beatle and Alphonse. But there'd been no answer, and he hadn't been able to figure out what Butch had thrown down. There wasn't much a rooster working on his own could do to get an answer, either. Sometimes it was tough being a chicken.

This was no time to go getting mopey. He'd need help. One thing Mr. Pepper definitely had going for him was his voice. He took in a big breath, then cock-a-doodled. To make his message clear to Jewel and Arabella, he crowed to the chorus of Beatle's hit single "Free Me."

It was pitch perfect! His chest feathers puffed with pride.

He looked up, tapping his clawed foot anxiously. Come on, come on, humans will soon be coming to investigate!

Soon enough, Jewel's head appeared in the window of the pet prison. "Hello, Mr. Pepper," she called.

"It's dangerous for you to be out there alone. Where's Esquire?"

"She's not with me at the moment," Mr. Pepper crowed. "I'll explain. Could you help me?"

"Don't come up; I'll come down," Jewel said, scanning the pool area. "Arabella's asleep, and all I've been doing is pacing this room, anyway." Jewel crawled out of the window and shut it behind her. She let herself down the curtain tassel, then plopped to the ground beside Mr. Pepper. "Phew," she said. "So—where's Esquire?"

Mr. Pepper opened and closed his beak, unsure of what to say. "She's with Butch."

"Trying to get the truth out of him?" Jewel asked hopefully.

"Something like that," Mr. Pepper replied. "Butch . . . approached the crevasse in secrecy. We caught him red pawed, but not before he dumped something down on Beatle."

Jewel's face darkened. "Oh! That doesn't sound good."

"No, it's not. The crevasse is already unstable, and I'm worried that Butch's goal was to make it even more so."

Jewel nodded, her expression tight. "It sounds like

Butch is our main suspect now."

Mr. Pepper glanced at her sideways, beak tilted. "Perhaps."

"Well, let's go see what we can do for my brother," Jewel said.

Mr. Pepper had thought of Jewel as soft and pampered, but she moved capably through the wilderness. Her foggy expression lifted, and there was a new energy to her movements.

"Hold on one second," Mr. Pepper said. Jewel came to a sudden stop, and suddenly Mr. Pepper's face was full of pangolin scales. He sputtered. "Before we leave the villa, I need to ask you about Arabella. She's the only one we haven't had a chance to—" Mr. Pepper's words broke off. Talking about Arabella had made him look back up at the villa window. It was *open* again. "I thought you said she was napping!"

"She *was* napping," Jewel said. "But I guess she woke up to open the window? Maybe it was stuffy in there."

"Or maybe she's sneaked out to tail us," Mr. Pepper said, looking around him suspiciously. "There's nothing to be done about it now. But let's keep alert."

The pangolin nodded somberly, and the pair stole toward the crevasse. It was just as Mr. Pepper had left it. There was still no answer from Beatle, no sign of

Alphonse, and no indication of what Butch's sabotage might have done.

"We'll get your brother out soon, I promise you," Mr. Pepper said. His words sounded sure. He only wished that he felt the same way. "I'd like to go check on him myself. I tried, though, and it wasn't the easiest thing in the world for a chicken to pull off."

Jewel stood beside him and peered down mournfully. "It's nothing pangolins are made for, either." Then her scales shook.

"What is it?" Mr. Pepper said.

"Don't look now," Jewel whispered. "But Arabella is approaching through the treetops. I can scent her at five o'clock."

Mr. Pepper cocked his head. Carnivores never realized that birds see best to their sides, not straight in front, and he often used that to his advantage. He could look for Arabella without her knowing he was looking. And there she was, hopping between the palm trees.

"Brace yourself," he whispered to Jewel. "She's approaching!"

But it turned out Arabella wasn't heading for them. She wasn't heading to the crevasse at all! She worked her way along the rocky path, down to the beach.

"Follow her," Mr. Pepper said. He didn't need to

ask twice. Jewel took the lead, moving low and silent through the sand and rocks.

Arabella moved fast through the treetops, but Jewel was able to keep on her scent. "What do you think she's up to?" Mr. Pepper huffed as they passed along the beach.

"I don't know," Jewel said, "but we're about to find out."

Mr. Pepper and Jewel hurried along the sand. Mr. Pepper was dazzled by the sunlight and couldn't move stealthily anymore. It was all he could do to keep oriented enough not to go right into the water! Jewel was much more capable, fortunately. She led them up the beach, then slowed.

Once Mr. Pepper had blinked away the purple glow the sun had left on his eyes, he saw a sad sight. Myrtle had wedged herself under a mangrove, eyes shut while the waves lapped her. She didn't look well. Not at all.

Unaware of Mr. Pepper and Jewel, Arabella descended from a nearby tree and approached the sea turtle. "Myrtle," she said, "I brought you a biscuit from the hotel room. Biscuits always make me feel better when I'm sick."

Myrtle slowly opened her eyes. "Oh, hello there. You said you would come back . . . and you did!"

Myrtle didn't seem interested in the biscuit, though.

She closed her eyes again.

Mr. Pepper couldn't help himself. Stealth be damned. He raced right up the beach to the sea turtle's side.

"What in the world?!" Arabella squealed, dropping the biscuit into the sand as she raced back up the palm tree in fright.

But Mr. Pepper had no attention for Arabella. Only for Myrtle. The rooster leaned down and listened to the sea turtle's breathing. Her eyes blinked heavily. "You're not well, Myrtle."

"It's that stomachache. It just keeps getting worse."

Arabella hooted and hollered from the top of the tree, throwing twigs down on them. "You can't sneak up on a monkey like that! You scared me half to death! Why were you following me?"

"*You* were following *us*," Jewel called up.

"I most certainly was not! I was just trying to do a good deed for Myrtle!"

"Hush, you two," Mr. Pepper said crossly. "Myrtle is very sick." He returned his attention to her. "Are you sure that was a jellyfish you ate?"

"Yes, I only eat jellyfish!" Myrtle replied.

"Which look a lot like balloons," Jewel said. "Dizzy likes to release them often at his parties."

"I love those balloons," Arabella said from the top of

the palm, resting her chin on her palm. Her anger had vanished. Monkey moods changed so quickly. "They're festive."

"They might be festive, but when they land in the sea, they look a lot like jellyfish," Jewel said. She laid a claw on Myrtle's back. "Mind if we take a closer look?"

Myrtle opened her mouth in response.

Mr. Pepper and Jewel peered in. A length of shiny ribbon trailed down her throat. "I recognize that," Mr. Pepper said. "I think it's—"

"Definitely from a balloon," Jewel said sourly. "I've seen plenty over the course of Dizzy's concerts."

"Ith really ate a baffoon?" Myrtle tried to say with her mouth open. "Thath really sthupid of me."

"Not at all. It looks just like a jellyfish when it's floating in the water. You can't be blamed. Now, hold on," Mr. Pepper said, trying to reach for the ribbon with his beak. It was too far back for him to get to, though.

"Let me," Jewel said. "This long snout and sticky tongue are useful."

"Hold still," Mr. Pepper said to Myrtle as he saw her wince in discomfort. "Only a minute longer."

Jewel reached her snout into Myrtle's mouth and wrapped her tongue around the balloon ribbon. She began backing up.

Myrtle cried out.

"Hold on, Myrtle," Mr. Pepper urged. "Just a few more pulls."

Arabella scampered down from the palm tree and looped her arms around Jewel's middle. Together, they pulled.

As Jewel and Arabella backed up, a gooey mylar balloon emerged—then another. And another. Finally there were four of them on the beach, all twisted together. As the last one emerged, the tension suddenly released from the ribbon. Jewel and Arabella went rolling along the sand.

Mr. Pepper inspected the nearest balloon. It read: Congratulations, Graduates! He shook his head. "I don't know why humans think releasing balloons is a good idea."

"I told you, it's good stagecraft!" Arabella said, and she brushed sand off her fur. She looked up to see the other three animals glaring at her and rushed to add, "But I can see the problem with it now!"

Myrtle closed her mouth, then opened it again. "Oh, wow," she said. "I feel much better. My stomach is gurgling, but in a good way."

Jewel made her way back to Myrtle. "Those balloons must have felt terrible."

Myrtle nodded. "I can't thank you enough."

"I have a favor to ask in return, only once you're feeling up to it," Jewel said.

"Of course," Myrtle said. "I'm up for anything. I'm one tough turtle."

Mr. Pepper gave her a shell a wing-pat.

"My brother is . . . still missing," Jewel said, "so I need to let all the animals know not to come to his concert tonight. I don't want to disappoint everyone."

Myrtle sighed. "Oh no. You must be so sad."

Jewel closed her eyes. "Numb is more like it. It hasn't sunk in yet."

"We're working to rescue Beatle," Mr. Pepper said. "There's still plenty of hope."

"The animals will be disappointed," Myrtle said. "We all love Beatle's music so much."

Jewel nodded.

Arabella bowed her head dramatically. "Could I have your attention, please?" she whispered. "I believe I've just had the idea of the century."

"Oh boy," Mr. Pepper muttered.

"I wonder," Arabella said, raising her head so the setting sun lit up her face in dramatic shadows, "if Jewel would consider giving a tribute concert instead? You could sing Beatle's songs, in his honor. He could hear them and be proud of you."

Mr. Pepper had been ready to shoot down whatever monkeybrained idea came out of Arabella's mouth, but this actually wasn't the worst plan he'd ever heard. "Beatle did say that he wanted you to go on in his place," he said gently to Jewel.

Her face fell. "I'm not the performer Beatle was. I'd disappoint him. If he can even hear me down there."

"I always listened for *your* voice in his songs," Mr. Pepper said. "It's so simple and so beautiful. Perfect for this situation. It will inspire your brother not to give up hope on us."

Jewel's eyes brightened, then she closed them. "No, I'm not up for it. I can't."

"We'll be there to support you, Jewel," Mr. Pepper said, scratching in the sand as he spoke, his eyes on the ground. Then he thought of something and crowed despite himself.

Jewel and Myrtle and Arabella looked at him, startled.

"Sorry," Mr. Pepper said. "It's just that I thought of something. If Beatle's stage collapse was the result of wrongdoing, then whoever did it clearly didn't want this concert to go forward."

"You're right; it's too dangerous," Myrtle said, nodding.

Arabella snapped her fingers. "I see where you're going with this! It might be all the more reason to go ahead. What a spectacle. The villain had some reason not to want the concert to occur—if it happens anyway, our adversary will be unable to resist coming, and maybe they'll bring themselves out into the open—"

"And we'll be ready for them!" Jewel finished triumphantly. "We can figure out once and for all who did this to my brother."

"It's probably Butch, and crossing a wildcat makes this a very risky plan, Jewel," Mr. Pepper said soberly. "He was clearly willing to go to great lengths to get Beatle out of the way. He might be willing to go to the same lengths to get you out of the way, too."

"I'm not worried about me," Jewel said. She looked up at Myrtle, Mr. Pepper, Arabella, the shining sea, and the villa on the hill. The idea of doing a memorial concert hadn't really moved her, but solving who had done this to Beatle clearly had. "I owe this to my brother. The show will go on."

Arabella clapped. "Art will triumph. Oh, this will be the story of the century!"

As Butch advanced on Esquire, she backed up far-ther into the closet, desperately thrashing her tail behind her to make sure she didn't trap herself in a corner. But it didn't hit a wall—instead it brushed some-thing warm and vibrating.

She turned to see computer equipment was stacked floor to ceiling in a small room off the walk-in closet. In the corner was a desk with a monitor. Butch jumped up on that desk and paced back and forth in front of the computer screen. "Here's where the footage is stored," he said.

"Footage?" Esquire asked, mind racing.

"The security footage of the villa. With a view of

the animal stage, if you know where to look. Why else
would we be in here?" Butch asked.

"Right, of course. Looking at footage. Sounds great."
Pulling her tail straight so it didn't scrunch beneath her,
Esquire took a seat in the desk chair, cracking her paw
knuckles. "Let's get started."

"You know what to do?" Butch asked, surprised.

"Of course," Esquire said. "Don't you know how to
work a computer?"

"No, I don't," Butch said.

"Well, then," Esquire said, suddenly quite proud of
herself. "Hmm. Where's the on switch?"

This computer took a while to wake up, not like the nice new one Esquire had back in the lair. She missed it dearly all of a sudden, her computer on its desk, a steaming cup of tea—and of course Mr. Pepper hopping around in the background.

While they waited for the computer to awaken, Esquire smiled tightly at Butch, returned to the computer screen, whistled, and looked around a bit. Finally it was ready. "Okay, great," she said. "Let's see. 'Ext.' That must be the exterior cameras. And we need, what, Thursday? Okay, I'll pick that, hold on here." Her claws tapped away at the keyboard.

True to cat form, Butch laid his head between his paws and proceeded to take a nap. Even though they were in a place where animals weren't supposed to be, engaging in illicit subterfuge. Felines!

There was a noise outside the room. A human voice. "Butch," Esquire hissed between clenched jaws. "Keep an eye out."

Butch yawned and pawed his eyes. Sometimes cats were truly worse than useless.

Esquire would have to finish this research before the human arrived. Her typing became even more frantic. "All right, let's see, Thursday. There are three cameras, why so many, let me start here, no, not that one, let's try number two. I can barely see anything, wait, whoops, that's because the monitor is too dark, here we go. Butch! Oh, look! There's the stage in the corner of the screen. It's a little grainy but I can see the iguanas working on the lighting, there's Arabella directing them. Butch, look lively!"

But Butch kept his eyes closed, leaving Esquire to see what happened next all on her own.

She leaned closer to the screen, eyes on Arabella. True to form, the director was bouncing on her tree-branch perch, ordering around the hutia roadies. The rodents scurried about, eagerly obeying, but the iguanas flicked their tongues in irritation. Could one of these animals have been the culprit, getting revenge against an overeager manager? Would Esquire have to interview dozens and dozens of rodents? She shuddered.

She leaned closer, eyes on the stage, watching the iguanas' claws. They were doing meticulous work, double-checking one another's fastenings, ensuring that everything was tip-top. There was a reason iguanas were highly sought after for this kind of work. Totally unflappable. Easier to be unflappable when you have nothing remotely resembling feathers, of course. Esquire hoped she remembered that observation to tell

Mr. Pepper when they got back together.

There! Off on the side of the screen, the shadows were shifting. Someone was approaching. Stealthily.

Casting an eye to Butch—who still had his eyes closed—Esquire leaned her head closer to the screen. Even in the low resolution of the security camera, she could make out the figure clearly. It stayed low to the ground, waiting until the iguanas were all focused on their construction before stalking closer. It went still whenever any of the lizards rotated one of its bulging eyes its way.

The sneaking intruder had a tail, two ears, glossy fur, and a collar that glinted in the stage lights.

It crept closer and closer to the stage, ducking its head beneath the platform and emerging with a bolt in its mouth. Taking a quick look around, it stalked away, then cast the bolt over the side of the cliff before disappearing into the darkness.

Esquire put her head in her paws, heart racing. She knew just who the culprit was now. He was sitting right beside her.

CHAPTER

Esquire clamped her paws over her snout so she wouldn't scream. She was locked in a room with the attempted murderer (or maybe the *actual* murderer!), with the animal that had cold-bloodedly sabotaged Beatle's stage and then returned to finish the deed. How was she going to get out of this pickle?

On top of that, there was the sound of human feet approaching, right outside the door.

That was what made Esquire lift her head from her paws. If the room's door was about to open, this might be her one chance to escape with her life. Better not waste it worrying!

As she looked up, she saw Butch's eyes were open

and glittering at her. "You realize why I can't have you poking around anymore, don't you?" he asked.

"You," Esquire spat. "You're the one who sabotaged Beatle's stage!"

Butch nodded, giving his foreleg a long lick. "I certainly did."

"It was just what it appeared to be—you were returning to the scene of the crime to finish the act. I never should have given you the benefit of the doubt." She was buying time, but she didn't know what miraculous escape plan she was possibly hoping for. She could hear the human's key card rattling in the lock.

"It was time you knew about the sabotage," Butch said. "You would have figured out the truth anyway. This way I'm in control of how you found out."

Esquire dashed past Butch and toward the hotel room door, every hair on her body rising.

Butch got to all fours, stretching his back, yawning wide to expose his sharp teeth. "You have been getting in my way from day one, fox. This plan would have gone off without a hitch if it hadn't been for you."

Esquire nearly jumped when her whiskers contacted the door sooner than she expected. Butch advanced on her, jaws open wide, a wicked smile on his face. "Don't be scared, Esquire. I'll make sure this all works out in a way that will be best . . . for all of us."

Esquire didn't even really know what Butch was implying, but it didn't sound like anything she wanted to see happen, not at all. She desperately longed for Mr. Pepper. Whenever she was at her wit's end, he always had one to spare for her. She cast an eye about the room. Maybe he'd sail in to save the day! But no. He was nowhere to be found. And the shutters were closed.

How had she been so foolish to assume that Mr. Pepper would understand that she was trying to get into Butch's good graces so he'd reveal himself? She'd failed both of them.

The room door opened.

Suddenly there were black boots on either side of Esquire. Some human started shouting in a deep voice, and Butch let out a whiny yowl.

"Butch? Oh, Butch! What's this wild animal attacking you!"

Esquire recognized that voice. She'd been nabbed by Dizzy Dillinger himself.

CHAPTER

14

"I wish I could help you with some of these colors," Mr. Pepper said, tapping the vials of nail polish with his beak. "I'm very handy with most things, but applying paint to scales is beyond any bird's skills, unfortunately."

"Butch would say that even the word *handy* is biased against other animals," Jewel said. "Only primates have hands, after all."

"Very true," Mr. Pepper said. "Unless you count clocks, of course." He paused. "I didn't realize Butch was so political."

"Butch is a surprisingly complicated cat," Jewel said as she sorted through the colors. The bottles tinkled as they knocked against one another. "What did Beatle always apply after Sunny Side Yellow? I can't remember."

"I think you should choose your own palette," Mr. Pepper sniffed. "You're your own artist, after all."

"That's true!" Jewel said. "In that case, I think I'll apply Periwinkle Blue next."

"That would look beautiful," Mr. Pepper said. "Not traditional rainbow order, but quite expressive."

"I could paint your toenails if you wanted!" Jewel said.

"Hmm!" Mr. Pepper said. "Is there a red that would match my coxcomb?" He shook his head. "We're getting

distracted. The sun is down, and you go on in just half an hour. There will be so many animals looking forward to your performance! Including Beatle himself, hopefully. How do you feel?"

"Oh, you know, weird, scared, nervous," Jewel said.

"All of those emotions make sense," Mr. Pepper said, nodding. "Are you sure you want to go ahead with this?"

"Yes," Jewel said. "I wouldn't want to let everyone down, not when they've traveled so far. And if there's a chance that this will help catch the culprit, I need to do it."

"You won't come to any harm," Mr. Pepper said. "I'll make sure of it! And we know your brother will be listening. This will give him hope."

Jewel let out a long sigh, looking at her multicolored scales. "This feels strange. I've never looked like Beatle before."

Arabella popped her head over the side of the nail polish chest, a nervous grin on her face. "That's because you're a star now, kid. Are you ready? We have to go on in just a few minutes!"

"Yes," Jewel said quietly, applying the finishing touches to her polish. "I think I'm ready."

"I'll lead the way," Arabella said, taking off at a

scamper. "Good thing all the humans are on the other side of the island listening to the Dizzy Dillinger concert, so we're not at risk of being observed. You can sing your heart out."

"We'll see about that," Jewel said.

"Come on, let's get a move on," Arabella said.

"Don't rush her," Mr. Pepper huffed. "She's an artiste! Arabella, you promise you've checked and double-checked the new platform?"

"Yes," Arabella said. "I jumped all over it. It's as sturdy as you can imagine."

"That's good," Jewel said.

"I'm so glad that you're doing this," Arabella prattled on. "After Beatle told me that he was going to retire, I was afraid that I'd never direct a show again."

Jewel and Mr. Pepper stopped in their tracks. "Retire? What do you mean, retire?" Jewel asked.

Arabella slowed and stopped. "Beatle never told you? He was done with the performing life. Ready for greener pastures and all that."

"No," Jewel said, shaking her head. "He didn't mention it."

"Oh," Arabella said. "Well, he was."

Jewel blinked heavily. "I don't understand. Why wouldn't he tell me something so important? I'm his sister. We tell each other everything."

Arabella paused. "Maybe he didn't tell you *because* you're his sister. Because he was worried that without him, you wouldn't have a music career." Seeing Jewel's crestfallen expression, Arabella hastened to add, "Not that I know anything for sure. I'm just tossing out ideas here."

"It's not true, though!" Jewel said. "I was only performing to help *him*!"

"Did you ever tell him that?" Mr. Pepper asked.

"No, not in those words. But he should have assumed it! Everyone knows he was more into performing than I was!"

"Maybe not. Sometimes people don't really know what's in our minds until we put it into words," Mr. Pepper said. His thoughts went to Esquire, who'd behaved so strangely around Butch. Had there been more to that than he'd known? Perhaps Mr. Pepper needed to take some of his own advice. Hmm.

He turned to Jewel. "Does this information change whether you want to go on?"

"Of course she's still going on!" Arabella squeaked.

"This is Jewel's decision!" Mr. Pepper squawked back. His mind was racing. If Beatle was going to retire, Arabella had manufactured a perfect situation to keep herself in the director's seat. The monkey had returned to being a suspect, as far as he was concerned.

"Yes, I'll still do it," Jewel said. "This could be what resolves the mystery of what happened to my brother. It could get us a step closer to saving him. Nothing matters more than that."

"You're a very brave pangolin," Mr. Pepper said. "Let's get going, then. Your audience awaits."

As they sneaked their way through the sandy trails leading from the villa, Mr. Pepper's thoughts returned to Esquire. She had her vain side, sure, but she was also an expert animal rescuer. Even in her most distracted state, she wouldn't have been *that* sidetracked by the fancy accessories in Dizzy's suite. What if she'd had her own plans underway, but she'd been unable to tell them to Mr. Pepper because Butch was there?

It was possible. It was very possible. He might have misjudged his dearest friend.

They could hear the murmurs of the waiting animals now, even if they couldn't see them. Two things were clear: there were a lot of animals in the audience, and they were very excited.

"I'll take the stage first, to let them know you'll be performing in Beatle's place, blah, blah, then you come up and sing, got it?" Arabella said.

Jewel gulped nervously. "I'm so glad you're here with me, Mr. Pepper."

"I wouldn't let you do this alone," Mr. Pepper clucked.

All the same, his thoughts went to that fool fox and what trouble *she* was undoubtedly getting into. Every feather on his body was telling him to go get her out of trouble. But Mr. Pepper had made a promise to Jewel, and the agency's reputation was on the line. Esquire would simply have to get out of whatever pickle she was in by herself.

Mr. Pepper mustered his courage. He was the sole representative of the Animal Rescue Agency on the scene, and he had a job to do.

The crowd of animals roared as Arabella took the stage.

CHAPTER

15

Esquire knew this might be her only chance to escape with her life. She turned and bolted between the human's legs. Between the legs of the famous Dizzy Dillinger himself! (That would make a good story someday if she survived this escapade.)

She never got a chance to see his face but did notice that he had very expensive sneakers, in a fun sort of neon green. By then she'd whizzed by and was out in the busy corridor.

There was shouting, feet running everywhere, stomping all around her, more shouting, one dead end, and a double-back amid shrieking humans, one of whom was Dizzy Dillinger himself. (They really were nice sneakers.) Then a housekeeper hurled a pile of dirty sheets at her—rude!—and Esquire ran through an empty expanse until, hissing with animal abandon, she finally made it to a hallway that ended in an open window. Imagining all sorts of angry humans (and a murderous wildcat) on her tail, Esquire launched herself through the gap without thinking twice.

Had she gone fast enough that none of them would notice she was wearing clothing? She could only hope. The ongoing secrecy of the Animal Rescue Agency depended on it.

She was in open air, legs outstretched, hurtling through space. Her legs ran on instinct, even though there was no ground beneath them. It was only a short drop until she was bouncing through palm fronds, from one tree to the next, coming to rest beside a nest of surprised seagull chicks. "Hi, good evening, sorry to disturb you," Esquire said, catching a chick who'd nearly tumbled out and snuggling it deep into the nest before scrambling through the fronds and down the trunk.

She whipped her head around. She'd gotten a little lost in all the commotion. Where was she? More importantly, where was Mr. Pepper? Esquire had to tell him and Jewel about the proof she'd discovered of Butch's wrongdoing, and *now*.

Then she heard Arabella's voice, amplified by the sound system. "Welcome, everyone! So great to see such a large crowd."

What was happening? Esquire took off toward the voice, careening through the scrub, her paws kicking up clouds of sand and dirt as she raced between palm trunks, over and under vegetation. The sound grew ever louder.

She started seeing evidence of a big animal crowd. Had Beatle gotten out, and was performing his concert after all? First up was a giraffe, an unusual sight indeed on a Caribbean island. "Wow, you certainly traveled a long way, didn't you, madame?" Esquire said as she rushed past, right by an anaconda (yipes) and a group of red pandas, nervously munching through sacks of bamboo-seed popcorn.

"Excuse me, sorry, coming through," Esquire said as she continued to weave her way. There was a surprisingly large herd of sheep, a dozing snapping turtle, two turtledoves (how cliché!), a whole lot of mice, a pod of bats (relatives of Alphonse, maybe, and no doubt wondering where their brother was; Esquire sincerely hoped she'd have some good news for them soon), and finally some sand lice, cheering away right at the front. Animals were very good about leaving the front seats for the littlest ones.

Now—where were Mr. Pepper and Jewel? And Beatle?!

Arabella was taking her time addressing the crowd from the stage, really milking the drama of the moment. Esquire caught only occasional words, as her focus was on working her way to the back of the performance space, scanning everywhere as she went. "The show must go on, though . . . yes, my friends, a new star has reluctantly come forward . . . with only a little bit of expert direction, she was ready."

What? Esquire picked up speed. Could it be that *Jewel* was going on? Esquire had to find her before she got on that stage—Butch was at large!

She'd worked her way to the other side of the stage . . . where she finally glimpsed Mr. Pepper, standing by Jewel.

When he saw her, he squawked and raced toward her. She lunged toward him, joining him midair, hugging her friend so hard they fell and rolled over the ground. It was all Esquire could do to make sure that they rolled away from the gaping crevasse.

"I'm sorry, Mr. Pepper!" she cried. "I didn't have a chance to explain. Butch is the culprit! I saw video proof. He did it all. He's probably near."

"No, *I'm* sorry!" Mr. Pepper said. "I let Butch's comments get under my skin, and I started to see you differently, but you're still Esquire; you're still my dear foolish Esquire Fox."

"Let's never fight again," Esquire said.

"Well, that's a foolish thing to wish for," Mr. Pepper said.

"Wait, are we fighting *already*?"

"Attention!" a voice hissed from the stage. It was Arabella. It seemed she'd just introduced the musical act, and the hutias had turned on the spotlights.

Stomach dropping, Esquire turned toward the stage, where Jewel had just arrived. It was too late. There was no hiding her away from Butch now.

CHAPTER

Mr. Pepper at her side, Esquire scanned the audience. The crowd was fidgety, talking among themselves. A razorbill booed. "That's not Beatle! We came for Beatle, not . . . whoever this is!"

Jewel's tail trembled as she took the stage, but she nonetheless faced bravely out. She squinted; she probably couldn't see much under the bright stage lights. Eyesight wasn't the strongest sense on a pangolin, anyway. It would be up to Esquire and Mr. Pepper to watch out for any attacker.

Jewel coughed and cleared her throat. It would already be hard to perform in her brother's place; Esquire could only imagine how much harder it would be to also be bait for a possible murderer.

"Boo!" said the razorbill. "You can't fool us!"

"Pipe down!" came a commanding voice. "Give her a chance."

The animals parted ways to reveal a sea turtle, right in their midst. "Myrtle—you're feeling better!" Jewel said.

"I am indeed," she said, smiling. "And you go right along and sing, dear. I'll make sure these animals around me behave." That shut the razorbill up. Most everyone listened to sea turtles.

Jewel opened her mouth.

She began to sing.

Esquire's jaw dropped.

Jewel had taken Beatle's dance hit "Let's Break the Scale" and slowed it down. Like his, her voice sounded like wind chimes. But while his were high and tinkly, hers were low and reedy. She didn't dance, didn't even budge; she just looked out at the audience and sang. It sounded like how a cool mountain stream feels.

Beatle's original song had been about a dance party that was so fun it broke the fun scales (an image Esquire never quite understood, to be honest), but to hear Jewel sing it, the song was a tribute to a party that never was. It was like a dreamy lullaby about fun. Esquire had never heard anything quite like it. Tears wet the corners of her eyes.

"Pay attention!" Mr. Pepper warned. "We're on the job, Esquire."

Esquire nodded. "Right. This is just so beautiful. Did you know she was going on tonight?"

"Yes. And we can thank her by keeping her alive."

"Well said, Mr. Pepper." Esquire patrolled the edge of the stage, eyes and ears alert. Luckily foxes can see well in low light, though the contrast with the stage lights was throwing her off. As far as she could tell, though, the animals were all motionless. Even the cranky razorbill was entranced.

Jewel finished her first song with a low hum, elongating the note until it winked out.

The crowd went wild, bounding to their feet, or into the air, or rolling in the sand if they had neither feet nor wings. Esquire saw a coyote and a macaw clutching each other and sobbing. There was so much movement that her eyes darted around, trying to catch it all. This would be the perfect moment for an evildoer to act. "Mr. Pepper, be on high alert!"

"I'm on it!" He hopped into the air, looking all around, then hopped again.

The crowd hushed as Jewel began to speak. "As you all know, my brother had an accident during the dress rehearsal. He fell down this very crevasse. I'm moved that you all came here anyway, and I hope that we can use this concert as a way to spread awareness, if any of you have a way to help get him out." Tears filled her eyes. "Maybe he can hear us. My next song is an original that I wrote over the last few days. It has a simple title. It's called 'Beatle, I Love You.' My brother, I hope you can hear it."

She began singing, again without accompaniment.

At least, not at first.

Esquire's sensitive ears picked up a grinding noise, coming from beneath the stage! She dropped to her belly and slithered under. This sabotage couldn't be happening again! But there it was—that grinding sound continued.

Esquire slithered forward, ears cocked. The new stage was bolted tight to the rock at multiple points, and the bolts all appeared firm. There was a vibration coming from the rock at the center, though, directly beneath where Jewel was performing. From the crevasse itself. "Mr. Pepper, do you sense—"

"I'm right behind you, Esquire," Mr. Pepper said. "This is very strange."

Esquire slunk toward the vibrating rock. Before her very eyes, a shape emerged from the depths! The shadowy figure was about the size of a house cat—or maybe a wildcat.

"Mr. Pepper! The enemy is emerging!" Esquire hissed.

She saw a flurry of feathers: Mr. Pepper was already backing out from the crawl space, probably heading to warn Jewel. Esquire squinted, trying to make out more of the culprit. But it was just too dark. It was only through her sensitive whiskers that she'd been able to pick up any sign of the intruder at all.

"Butch!" she hissed. "Is that you?!"

The figure paused, but there was no answer. Then it scrambled out of the crevasse and toward the back of the stage.

"Oh no you don't," Esquire said as she scrambled the other way. She'd get to Jewel first, she'd be sure of it, to stop her from meeting the same end as her brother.

Esquire barreled over the sandy rocks, banging her head on the bottom of the stage, finally emerging and whipping around to check on Jewel. She was bathed in soft light, lost in her beautiful song.

"I'll save you!" Esquire screamed, careening toward her, soon blinded by the stage lights. Jewel had a split second to look at her, terrified, before fox and pangolin rolled together, right off the stage.

The crowd was roaring and screeching, but Esquire couldn't see them, just swirls of color as her face filled with Jewel's painted scales. Together they rolled, over and over, before they came to rest under a palm tree. "Are you okay?" Esquire asked, leaping to her back paws. "Did he get you?"

"What are you talking about?" Jewel asked. "Of course I'm okay. Why wouldn't I be okay?"

"Because, because . . ." Esquire sputtered. She blinked under the stage lights.

Hundreds of animals were staring at them. At her. Because she'd just ruined Beatle's tribute concert.

"Wait, is that Esquire Fox, from the Animal Rescue Agency?" the giraffe loudly whispered.

"Oh, great," Esquire muttered. "*Now* everyone recognizes me."

"Hush, I'm sure there's some sense to all this," Myrtle said. "Esquire, what's gotten into you?"

Esquire filled with a strange mix of pride and shame. "Oh my gosh," she said, tears darting her eyes. "I must have been mistaken. I'm so sorry, Jewel."

The animals began to boo.

"My apologies, everyone!" Esquire said to the crowd. She put her paws on Jewel's front shoulders. "Please start the song over."

Jewel looked around, up and into the stage lights, confused beyond words.

"There's no need for her to perform anymore, not if it's to bring out the culprit," came Mr. Pepper's calm voice as he took the stage. "Because there they are!"

He pointed a claw at the far edge of the stage, where the shadowy figure was just emerging into the spotlight.

Myrtle's voice carried over the crowd's roar. "How can this be?"

"I don't understand!" Mr. Pepper said, feathers fluffing.

There was an emu in front of her, so Esquire couldn't get a good view of the stage. She gripped Jewel's paw and moved with her, around the emu, so they could see who had captured the crowd's attention.

Jewel gasped.

"Oh, wow," Esquire said.

It was Beatle.

He'd clearly had a rough time of it. The pangolin was much skinnier than he'd ever been on his album covers, his scales raised and cracked when once they'd been smooth and moisturized. He looked like a walking pine cone. There were some traces of his trademark rainbow nail polish, but only deep in the crevices. The rest was back to its natural pangolin color.

Jewel lifted herself to all fours, mouth hanging open in shock. "You're . . . you're . . ."

"I'm alive," Beatle said simply. "I've been hiding away in a little cave I prepared for myself down there. I could have climbed out whenever I wanted. I'm so sorry, Jewel."

The crowd of animals had been silent before, but now they started murmuring. Esquire watched a red panda in the back row lose his mind over the drama, mouthing, "What is *happening*?" to the rest of the pandas, who were munching their bamboo-seed popcorn faster than ever.

As the murmurs rose, Beatle looked out at the audience, as if he only just now noticed them. "And I'm sorry to all of you. For tricking you."

"I bet you are," the razorbill grumbled loudly.

"But why?" Jewel asked softly as she made her way onto the stage. She squinted into the spotlights. "Why would you pretend to be trapped away?"

Before her brother could answer, Jewel had nuzzled close to him, pressing her throat against his. "Whatever your answer is, I'm so glad you're okay," she continued.

"I owe you an explanation," Beatle said to his sister. "I owe everyone an explanation, but especially you."

He stepped to the front of the stage, using a claw to shield his eyes from the key chain LEDs. "Could you turn off the stage lights, please?"

The hutias and iguanas looked over at Arabella, who was watching the proceedings from the top of a nearby palm. She was so absorbed that she startled when she realized everyone was staring at her. "You heard him, get those lights turned out!"

Rodents and lizards swarmed into the trees as the crew rushed to do the director's bidding.

Beatle waited patiently while the lights went out, one by one. Jewel was by his side. Esquire could only imagine what was going through her head, but the main emotion on her face appeared to be relief. Her brother was alive!

Once the stage lights were out, natural moonlight lit the venue in muted colors. The crowd calmed, and their murmurs quietened.

Beatle cleared his throat. "I guess you could say that I . . . I felt trapped. Everyone assumed I was living the dream, but I'd never asked to be a performer. I'd been in the jungle, living my natural life, when I was taken. I've come to realize that's what it was, that I was *taken*. I was just a baby when it happened, so all I can really remember is my life on the road with Dizzy Dillinger. But I must have been in the jungle with other pangolins, right? Don't I have a right to that life if I want it?"

"Like in my dream," Jewel whispered. "You started remembering our childhood, too!"

Beatle stopped speaking and just sat right where he was on the stage, head in his claws. Jewel sniffed the ground tentatively, then curled herself protectively around him.

The animals started murmuring again. "Can someone tell me what is actually going on here?" the red panda in the back screeched. "I'm so confused!"

Esquire took to the stage, rubbing her paws together. "I think I might be able to explain. Esquire Fox of the Animal Rescue Agency here, for those who don't know me." She waited for applause, but when none came she hurried onward. She'd just have to come to terms with the fact that she was small potatoes in this world of pop superstars. "Beatle has always performed for us because he thought that's what we wanted, but no one ever asked him what *he* wanted. He doesn't want to be a star anymore. He wants to be a natural-living pangolin."

Jewel stepped back from her brother. "And you thought I *did* want this performing life? You faked your death so that I would have to take over?"

Beatle lifted his head slowly and nodded. "I knew you would say no if I asked you, but if I just disappeared you would step forward. I thought I could give this life to you. Wasn't that what you always wanted?"

Jewel shook her head. "No, it's not. And you should have asked me. No one asked me what *I* wanted, either."

Beatle nodded. "I just assumed. From the way everyone treated me, I thought everyone wanted this life, and I was the crazy one to hate it. But maybe no one is meant for it. I'm sorry, Jewel. I was too wrapped up in myself to even consider that this wasn't what you wanted."

Esquire began to pace the stage, tapping her chin with her claw. She was busy figuring out what was actually happening, right in front of this watching crowd. It was pretty exhilarating. She could get the appeal of performing. "Let me see if I can help explain further, Beatle. You knew you would have to wait until Dizzy's retinue departed tomorrow morning for you to make your getaway," Esquire said, making sure her voice was loud enough for the animals in the back to hear. "All you needed was a little . . . assistance."

Esquire could hear a cat's yowl from within the crowd. Wherever he was, Butch knew what she was about to say. Esquire was on a roll now! "Butch, come forward," she intoned.

The wildcat clearly had no intention of showing himself. Esquire continued her speech. "Butch the wildcat helped rig the stage so it would give way during your dress rehearsal. Then he delivered supplies to you, so you could survive the wait. That was food that he dropped into the crevasse!"

Beatle nodded. "I'd set up a little chamber for myself down there, with water and a coloring book. I've been living there for days, waiting for Dizzy's party to be over so I could start the journey home."

"Were you even going to say goodbye to me?" Jewel asked, tears in her voice.

Beatle didn't have any words to respond with. He just stared at the ground.

Mr. Pepper hopped onto the stage. "Let's let you two talk about this in private. This isn't a public sibling show for everyone to gawk at." He squawked toward the crowd, waving his wings. "Go on, get home. This performance is over. There are no more Beatle the Pangolin performances in your future."

The crowd looked at one another, aghast. The flamingo cried out in horror at the loss.

"One moment," Beatle said. He turned to his sister. "I don't expect anything from you. I have no right to. But I wonder if you might be willing, one last time, for the sake of all the animals who have come so far—"

"To perform with you?" Jewel finished.

Beatle nodded. "I'm ashamed to even ask it."

"We'll talk after," Jewel said. "But yes. My answer is yes."

The crowd's murmuring turned into roars and caws of approval. A praying mantis gave a loud whistle, even more impressive given his small size. Esquire hadn't even known that praying mantises *could* whistle, to be honest.

"How about 'Love Is the Stickiest Tongue'?" Beatle asked. Jewel nodded.

Beatle stood at the front of the stage, and Jewel took her usual place behind him. Beatle shook his head. "No, not in the background. Up here with me. We're performing this as a duet. The way we should have been performing all along."

Shyly, Jewel made her way downstage. She stood beside her brother, taking in the adoring crowd. Then she nodded.

They began to sing.

CHAPTER

Esquire was not the superstitious sort, but for the few minutes the pangolins were singing, she found herself believing in magic. There was no better word to describe the experience. The ordinary world cracked open, and something truly extraordinary emerged. Not the lyrics—those were never Beatle's strong suit—but the emotion and love pouring between the two siblings that was lifted and sent flying by their harmonies.

Even Mr. Pepper was overcome by the end, dabbing at his eyes with the hem of his strawberry apron.

Beatle and Jewel performed no fewer than four

curtain calls. The applause never died down; Jewel just eventually insisted that the crowd let her lead her exhausted and underfed brother off the stage. The crowd started to follow, wanting to meet the stars, but Esquire and Mr. Pepper worked as bouncers, keeping them at bay so the pangolin siblings could get away.

Fireworks had started going off on the other side of the island, too—a sign that Dizzy Dillinger's concert had just finished. The animals would have to disperse before humans started wandering the island again. "Back to your homes, everyone, back to your homes ASAP!" Arabella called out, shooing the red pandas away from the stage.

One especially avid wildebeest wanted to get his backside signed by Beatle and Jewel and was intent on making it through to the celebrities despite Esquire's and Mr. Pepper's best efforts. A loud hiss brought him to a stop. One look at the bared teeth of the wildcat emerging from the darkness was enough to send the overexcited fan scattering.

"Thanks for coming to the concert!" Esquire called out after his departing tail. She turned to Butch. "And thanks for the help. I'm sorry I suspected you."

"You were perfectly correct to suspect me," Butch said. "I *was* tricking you, after all. Just to help Beatle, not hurt him. But how could you know that?"

"An unexpected motive! That was the only wrinkle stopping me from solving the case," Esquire said. Her claim inspired a ruffled cheek feather from Mr. Pepper, his equivalent of a raised eyebrow.

"Now we just need to find Alphonse," Esquire said, looking mournfully down into the crevasse.

Butch lowered his nose to the ground. "Do you mean your bat field agent? He's fine. I'll bring you to him. Follow me."

"Oh, thank goodness!" Esquire said.

Butch tapped his nose on the ground, then stole along the edge of the crevasse, before coming to a stop. He checked a marking on the ground, making sure he was in the perfect position. Then he stepped right into the void!

Esquire and Mr. Pepper rushed to the edge of the hole and looked down. "Hello?!"

"Come on down," Butch called up from the darkness. "You'll see it's a soft landing."

"Hmm," Esquire said. It was just impenetrable blackness below, from what she could see. Butch might not be a suspect anymore, but she wasn't quite ready to go doing trust exercises with him yet.

"I'll go first," Mr. Pepper said. "Chickens can fall most any distance safely." He hopped into the crevasse.

"Come on down!" he clucked up a few seconds later. "But make sure you're right on the marking where Butch was standing when he stepped in."

Esquire lined herself up with a small X that the cat had scratched in the rock. Then she held her nose, as if she were jumping into a lake, and stepped off the edge.

It was only a short fall before she hit a burlap cushion and bounced. She came to all fours in a rough-hewn chamber. In one corner were a few bricks of dirt, swarming with ants. Beatle's food. In another was a jug of water. In the middle, beside the burlap cushion, was a flickering candle next to a coloring book with some crayons. That was about it.

"So this is where Beatle was hiding away all this time," Mr. Pepper said. "Interesting."

Beatle and Jewel emerged from the shadows. "This was all you were going to bring with you when you escaped?" Jewel asked. "Just some ants and water?"

"And a coloring book," Beatle said quietly. "I do like colors."

"It *is* very surprising!" Esquire said. "You have access to all the riches of Dizzy Dillinger. You could be the wealthiest animal in the world, could have all the fancy clothing and gadgets you wanted, but you've got next to nothing here." He didn't even nab those sequined flip-flops from the walk-in animal clothes closet. It was all giving her a lot to think about.

"Pangolins in the jungle don't have *any* belongings," Beatle answered. "Just the scales on their backs. At least I think that's how it works. I've never met any wild pangolins."

"An animal can take as many clothes or items around with them as they wish," Mr. Pepper said, looking at Esquire. "It's not our place to judge their choices. The important thing is that they have the freedom to choose. That's the whole purpose of the Animal Rescue Agency, isn't it, Esquire? To give as many animals as possible the sort of freedom that you and I have."

Freedom. Helping each animal live its natural life. Not fancy party invites. Esquire had gotten a little sidetracked. "Thanks, friend," Esquire said, straightening her jacket. "I needed that reminder."

"And thank *you* for all your help," Jewel said to Esquire and Mr. Pepper.

"Of course," Esquire said. "Now, about our field agent."

"She's referring to that bat," Butch explained, as he emerged from the shadows to stand beside the pangolins.

"Oh, him?" Beatle said. "I'm sorry about that. He

found me easily, but I couldn't have him giving away that I was safe and sound down here." Beatle rummaged behind him, then returned with Alphonse. The little bat had been bound up tight, a palm frond covering his mouth. Beatle delicately removed it.

"Let me go!" Alphonse said, wriggling. "Why, you big bully, I was trying to *rescue* you, and you, you go and tie me up!"

"I'm very, very sorry," Beatle said.

"I'm sorry, too, Alphonse," Esquire said. "You went through more than I ever intended you to on this mission."

Once he'd been fully untied, Alphonse seemed to calm some, pulling his key ring belt up with great dignity. "I suppose it's all part of the risk of being a field agent," he said. "Now, do you think I might eat some of those ants? I'm starving!"

"Be my guest," Beatle said. Alphonse tucked into the insect feast.

"We know Beatle is heading into the wilds. But what do *you* want to do now?" Mr. Pepper asked Jewel.

She looked startled. "I don't know! I haven't really thought about it."

"Maybe it's time to start thinking about what *you*

want, not just what others want for you," the rooster said gently.

"Yes, I think you're right, Mr. Pepper," she said.

"If you want to take over performing, the animals would love it," Butch said. "Arabella and I can help you until you've learned all the ropes."

Jewel smiled. "That's very kind of you. But this performing life isn't right for me, either. I've been having the same dreams Beatle's been having. So many greens in the leaves, dappled sunlight, flavors of ant that I've never tasted before—"

"You, too?" Beatle exclaimed. "I've been having those for weeks, which was when I started to want to leave."

"It sounds like maybe you'd both like to travel to Java, to discover your roots," Mr. Pepper said.

The pangolin siblings looked at each other, then nodded in unison.

"Maybe *you'd* consider singing for the animal world, instead of us?" Beatle asked Butch.

The cat yowled and placed a paw over his face, suddenly shy. "I don't know about that," he whispered.

"You'd be great," Esquire lied. Everyone knew the unfortunate truth about cat voices.

Mr. Pepper clucked to get back everyone's attention. "If you do wind up relocating to Java, we need an Indonesian representative. Perhaps, Jewel, you would consider doing us the great honor of—"

"Being the Animal Rescue Agency's Indonesian agent?" Jewel exclaimed. "I'd love to!"

Mr. Pepper nodded. "This is very good news indeed. Now there just remains the matter of billing."

Esquire draped a paw over Mr. Pepper's shoulder. She truly hated this topic. "These siblings have been through a lot. I'm sure they want to have a night's rest, down here in this secret cave where they won't be found by that animal catcher or any other humans. Let's discuss any little details of this rescue arrangement in the morning."

"But, but—" Mr. Pepper sputtered.

"Beatle," Esquire asked. "Would you consider joining Jewel in the field as our representative?"

Beatle nodded, eyes shining. "I'd be honored."

Mr. Pepper cock-a-doodled as he produced two slips of paper from a pocket of his apron. Contracts.

"Did you have those at the ready this whole time?" Esquire asked.

"Just in case!" Mr. Pepper said.

"You really are amazing," Esquire said, giving her

chicken friend a big hug, lifting him high into the air while the pangolin siblings placed their paw prints on the dotted lines.

"That is quite true," Mr. Pepper wheezed. "Now please put me down."

CHAPTER

"Myrtle, I wonder if you'd be willing to slow down?" Esquire called out, giving the sea turtle shell beneath her a sharp rap with her knuckle.

"Why would you want her to do that?" Mr. Pepper said, turning over so the Caribbean sun could warm the other side of his beak.

"I'm not sure I'll ever again achieve this peak level of happiness, so I want this journey home to last as long as possible." To make her point, Esquire took a long sip of her drink—a sort of frozen pineapple slush that Arabella had concocted for them as a parting gift.

"I guess you might be right," Mr. Pepper said, taking a sip of his own drink. He had a smaller cup, made from

the fragment of a coconut shell. Arabella had sprinkled his with poppy seeds to make it more appetizing to a chicken's palate. It was very considerate of her, considering they'd been interrogating her as a suspect just a few days before.

They reclined over the shell, scents of Esquire's coconut tanning oil and Mr. Pepper's lemon oil furniture polish wafting over them. Gentle waves from the crystal-blue sea lapped against Myrtle's green back. All the while, the sea turtle's strong strokes brought them farther and farther from the island's shore. She'd recovered her strength once Mr. Pepper and Jewel extracted the balloons from her belly—and they'd checked that very morning that her eggs were safe, which gave her some extra pep.

Esquire was glad to see that Mr. Pepper was finally wearing his puffy bathing suit, the one made from the old-timey handbag. It looked wonderful on him.

"Could I borrow those back?" Esquire asked Mr. Pepper, plucking their binoculars from the chicken. He never used them correctly, anyway, always pointing them in the wrong direction. They were actually children's opera glasses, but they served their purpose very nicely. Esquire placed them up to her eyes, adjusting the focus so she could see the mangroves at the edge of Dizzy's private island.

There on the beach were two pangolins in adventuring gear. Their scales were back to their natural color. Jewel had an explorer's helmet on her head, Beatle had a utility belt around his waist (as much as a pangolin has a waist, which is to say not much at all), and they were holding a map up to their noses, clearly disagreeing about which way to go. Esquire had been very impressed with how levelheaded Jewel turned out to be and was confident they'd find their way to Java eventually.

"This is a first, two new field agents from one mission," Esquire said. "And no one to add to the villain wall!"

"Let's not get complacent," Mr. Pepper clucked. "There are plenty of villains out there still causing trouble."

"That's very true, Mr. Pepper," Esquire said, chastened. She took a big sip of her pineapple drink. "I'm sure we'll be saving the day again before we know it. But that doesn't mean we can't celebrate any victories that come our way."

"That's very true," Mr. Pepper said. He took a sip

of his own drink, and his eyes brightened. "Just think how many resources those pangolins had, being the exotic pets of a human megastar. This must have been an excellent mission as far as billing."

Esquire lowered her drink to her lap and took a deep breath. "Yes, about that, Mr. Pepper—"

"With all this new funding, maybe our two new agents could help us start an Asia bureau!" Mr. Pepper said excitedly. "I've been thinking for a while that our headquarters are simply too far away for us to get to the other side of the world in time to be much help. What do we do if we get a call from an animal in danger in Pakistan or Mongolia, say? This Asia bureau will be wonderful. I'll have to get those local moles to start gnawing some new letter blocks to print us up revised letterhead—"

"You see, Mr. Pepper, about that. I brought up billing to the pangolins, I really did, I remembered—"

"Of course you remembered. No fox is harebrained enough to make *that* mistake again, not after that catastrophe in the Arctic. All we got out of that were some questionable arts and crafts and a few wet envelopes, if you'll remember. Horrors."

"Erm, yes, so when I did talk to them, finally, Jewel had a surprising answer. A concerning one, even, I guess you could call it."

Mr. Pepper nodded wisely. "Was it the logistics problem? I've thought about that, too. It can be hard to transport that much wealth and goods, particularly when the pangolins wanted to get away as quietly as possible. What I figure is, we approach a whale willing to haul a net for us, and then we—"

The tension was just too much. Esquire's body jerked, sending her drink flying into the ocean. "Blast," she said mournfully. "I wasn't finished with that."

Mr. Pepper watch the drink splash into the sea, then looked at Esquire. His eyes narrowed.

"There isn't any billing!" Esquire finally managed to say, the words coming out in one gasp. "That's what I'm trying to say."

Mr. Pepper's coxcomb stood straight up. "What do you mean, 'there isn't any billing'?"

"So," Esquire said, her heart racing as she smoothed her jacket. "What I *mean* is, is that, I told Jewel just what you *told* me to tell our new friends, I mean clients, that a rescue agency can only run by billing the animals it rescues, and she agreed entirely, and that's when she mentioned that Arabella made amazing pineapple drinks."

"You accepted *pineapple drinks* as payment?" Mr.

Pepper said, his voice rising into a cock-a-doodle-doo. It would have been intimidating if he weren't wearing a handbag.

"No, no, let me finish. That was when Arabella started making us these drinks—which really are quite amazing, don't you think? At least they were before I went and spilled mine—and Jewel explained that yes, she did have lots of beautiful things to donate to us to help with operating costs, and Beatle did, too, but that they were already planning on doing something *else* with all those resources."

"They're going to be living in the lap of luxury off in Indonesia?" Mr. Pepper said. He'd started pacing Myrtle's shell. On top of everything else, now Esquire was nervous that her best friend in the whole world was about to tumble into the sea.

"No, nothing like that," she said. "They're starting a charity dedicated to the prevention of wild animal trafficking. They want to stop other young animals from being captured and sold as pets."

"We just saw them heading off into the mangroves, on their way to Indonesia. They had nothing with them. Where *are* all these supposed resources?"

"Beatle and Jewel might have escaped, but Butch and

Arabella are staying with Dizzy. They'll be siphoning wealth off forever, directing it to the pangolins' charity. It seems fitting that Dizzy will be the one paying for the prevention of pangolin trafficking. It's all pretty ingenious, if you ask me. Now stop pacing, would you? You're making me nervous."

Mr. Pepper returned to the middle of the shell and harrumphed as he sat down, the bathing suit riding up in the process so it covered his face. "It's all wonderful for *them*. We're the ones returning from a long-distance mission with only a couple of pineapple drinks to show for it. Make that *one* pineapple drink, now that you managed to toss yours into the sea."

"You are also coming home with *me!*" cried a small voice from the breast pocket of Esquire's linen jacket. "I am very excited to visit the home base. You will find a bat very useful."

"We're excited to have you stay with us, Alphonse," Esquire said, using a pinkie claw to pat his tiny head.

Esquire could just see the visible frill of coxcomb wobble as Mr. Pepper shook his head within the handbag. She tugged down the fabric so she could see her friend's face. "I'm not happy with this turn of events," he grumbled. "We cannot run a business without billing!

You of all animals should know that, Esquire."

Esquire lay back, enjoying the coconut scent that rose from her sun-lightened fur. "We'll get by, Mr. Pepper. We always do."

"Only because I manage to make every little scrap we have stretch as far as possible," Mr. Pepper huffed. "Who darns all your socks over and over?"

"You do, Mr. Pepper, and I'm very grateful," Esquire said. "I know fox claws are murder on socks." She reclined even farther, forelegs behind her head, closing her eyes so the sun could warm her eyelids. The rhythm of Myrtle's steady strokes through the water was very relaxing. Still, she wished she had her pineapple drink to sip.

"For example, I can make this go a little further, too."

Esquire cracked open an eye. Mr. Pepper was holding out one clawed foot. In it was his precious small pineapple drink, poppy seeds floating on top. "Take mine. I insist."

Unexpected tears came to Esquire's eyes. "Mr. Pepper, I couldn't. Well, if you insist, one small taste."

She leaned forward and took a delicate sip from the paper straw. Then she lay back. Life with Mr. Pepper was strange, and unexpected, but it was wonderful all the same.

"Now can we just enjoy the journey home?" Esquire asked sleepily, rocked by the waves.

She felt a ruffle of feathers at her side as Mr. Pepper nestled in beside her. "Yes," the rooster said. "I do think we deserve that."

To each animal,
the right to live a natural life

Haha, yippee!!! It says "Esquire Fox" up there, but this is not Esquire Fox, no way, this is ALPHONSE THE BAT! The best of all the agency representatives, without a single doubt!! Esquire is supposed to type up field notes for each mission, but she hates doing it, so she was dragging her paws, and I LOVE being HELPFUL so I've logged in and I'm typing away while Esquire naps! She's going to be so happy that I've done it for her! Mr. Pepper will not be happy, but he's asleep, too, so lalalalalalalalalala!!!

First note: bats are the best!!!!

Second note: balloons are the worst!!!! Seriously. Just don't use them. It's already pretty bad if humans have some for a party and then throw them out. That means they will sit in a landfill for thousands of years, wah, wah, bad news. It's worse if ~~their there~~ they're released for a party or something. Then they fly into the sky, and all the humans ooh and aah and all the animals go oh no, because you know what? What goes up must come down, and those balloons will deflate and fall into the ocean. An empty balloon looks just like a jellyfish, which means a fish or a turtle or a whale might eat it and can't digest it and then it fills up their belly and they can't eat their normal food anymore and they *die*. All because a human thought releasing balloons would be pretty. Nuh-uh, NO FAIR AT ALL, HUMANS, what are you thinking, I thought you all declared that you were sooooo smart!!!

Third note: Aren't pangolins the cutest? Except when they tie you up and gag you, but I'm getting over that because those SCALES are SO PRETTY. Pangolins are sweet natured and love to eat all sorts of insects, although they specialize in ants. There are many different species of pangolins, and they live in Asia and also sub-Saharan Africa. Unfortunately some humans think their scales have medical properties (spoiler: they do not!!!) so they're highly trafficked, which doesn't mean they're stuck on highways; it means people kidnap them from the wild. Some of them wind up as pets, and some wind up as medicine or food (yuck).

Animal trafficking leads to the deaths of hundreds of thousands of animals each year, which is bad enough, but it also endangers humans! There are some diseases that are zoonotic, which means they pass from animals to humans. I looked it up. When humans bring wild animals into markets, they're risking introducing viruses or bacteria or parasites into the human population, which can have really serious consequences for the human world. Or so I hear.

Mr. Pepper always insists on reputable sources, so here are some articles you can read for more information:

"Why the Balloon Release Tradition
Is Terrible for the Environment,"
Forbes,
www.forbes.com

"What Is a Pangolin?"
World Wildlife Fund,
www.worldwildlife.org

"Illegal Trade in Pangolins Keeps Growing as
Criminal Networks Expand,"
National Geographic,
www.nationalgeographic.com

Ack! Mr. Pepper is up! Byebyebyebyeseeyoulater youdidn'tseemehere.

Love,

Alphonse

FROM THE KITCHEN OF MR. PEPPER:

FROZEN PINEAPPLEADE

Note that this recipe involves a knife and a blender, so juvenile animals—like pups and kittens and tadpoles—must get an adult's help to make this.

(Unless you're a sea cucumber and can just regrow any limbs you cut off, in which case slice away! Although . . . if you *are* a sea cucumber, you'll find it difficult to operate the blender.)

INGREDIENTS:
- 4 limes
- ¼ cup sugar
- ¼ cup water
- 3 cups frozen pineapple chunks (If you have fresh pineapple, cut it up, put it in a bag, and place it in the freezer for a few hours. You can also just buy frozen pineapple.)
- 1 cup ice cubes
- Some sort of small seed, like poppy or sesame, if you're serving this drink to birds.

STEPS:

- If you have a grater, use it to grate the skin off two of the limes. Humans call this lime zest. It's optional.
- Roll the limes back and forth on the counter. This makes them release more juice and feels good under your chicken feet.
- Juice the four limes. This should give you about half a cup of juice.
- Place the zest, juice, sugar, and water in the blender, and blend until you no longer see any sugar crystals. (Make sure Esquire isn't napping first, because she does not like to be woken up by blender noise.)
- Add some frozen pineapple and blend, then add more and blend, a little at a time. Do not try to blend it all at once, or you will spend two days cleaning the lair's ceiling.
- Blend in the ice the same way. If the drink looks watery, blend in even more ice. If it looks too thick, blend in more water.
- Pour into cups.
- Optional: Sprinkle small seeds on top before serving. This is how birds prefer their frozen drinks.

(Thanks to human chef Kate Merker
for her help with this recipe!)

ACKNOWLEDGMENTS

Many thanks to the humans who made this book happen, especially to my extraordinary editor, Ben Rosenthal. Thanks as well to my agent, Richard Pine, and the entire team at Katherine Tegen Books, including my publicist, Mitch Thorpe, production editor Laura Harshberger, and copyeditor Sarah Chassé. I'm grateful, too, to those who gave me feedback on Esquire's and Mr. Pepper's story: Eric Zahler, Daphne Benedis-Grab, Donna Freitas, Marie Rutkoski, Marianna Baer, Jill Santopolo, Anne Heltzel, Anna Godbersen, and Barbara Schrefer.